PRAISE
ONLY THE DEVIL IS HERE

"I burnt through *Only the Devil Is Here* in one fevered night. Stephen Michell is the real, raw deal: a fierce young writer with chops and heart."
—Nick Cutter, bestselling author of *The Troop* and *The Acolyte*

"*Only the Devil Is Here* is a gripping, cinematic supernatural thriller, shot through with unsettling imagery and startling insights into the nature of good and evil. Suspenseful, scary and unexpectedly moving, it's a wild ride from start to finish."
—David Demchuk, Giller Prize-nominated author of *The Bone Mother*

"With *Only the Devil Is Here*, Stephen Michell announces himself as a new and powerful presence on the literary horror scene. This is curt, violent, poetic storytelling, a Cormac McCarthyesque journey from darkness into even deeper darkness, suffused from moment one on with gothic nighttime awe and terror, yet also shot through with the slimmest threads of hope—intimations of numinosity, if not of salvation. For all you probably won't like where it takes you, it's just so damn hard to turn away."
—Gemma Files, Shirley Jackson Award-winning author of *Experimental Film*

"An outstanding literary horror debut, the lean, muscular prose of which barely contains the bursting, profoundly human heart of the novel. *Only the Devil Is Here* is the work of a natural storyteller at the start of what will doubtless be a very long, very promising career."
—Michael Rowe, author of *October, Enter, Night,* and *Wild Fell*

ONLY THE DEVIL IS HERE

ONLY THE DEVIL IS HERE

STEPHEN MICHELL

FIRST EDITION

Distributed in Canada by
Fitzhenry & Whiteside Limited
195 Allstate Parkway
Markham, Ontario L3R 4T8
Phone: (905) 477-9700
e-mail: bookinfo@fitzhenry.ca

Distributed in the U.S. by
Consortium Book Sales & Distribution
34 Thirteenth Avenue, NE, Suite 101
Minneapolis, MN 55413
Phone: (612) 746-2600
e-mail: sales.orders@cbsd.com

Library and Archives Canada Cataloguing in Publication

Michell, Stephen, 1990-, author
    Only the devil is here / Stephen Michell. -- First edition.

Issued in print and electronic formats.
ISBN 978-1-77148-434-3 (softcover).--ISBN 978-1-77148-435-0
(ebook)

    I. Title.

PS8626.I27O55 2017   C813'.6   C2017-907119-X
                                            C2017-907120-3

CHIZINE PUBLICATIONS
Peterborough, Canada
www.chizinepub.com
info@chizinepub.com

Edited by Sandra Kasturi & Samantha Beiko
Proofread by Leigh Teetzel

Canada Council   Conseil des arts
for the Arts   du Canada

We acknowledge the support of the Canada Council for the Arts which last year invested
$20.1 million in writing and publishing throughout Canada.

ONTARIO ARTS COUNCIL
CONSEIL DES ARTS DE L'ONTARIO
an Ontario government agency
un organisme du gouvernement de l'Ontario

Published with the generous assistance of the Ontario Arts Council.

Printed in Canada

Dedicated to my dad
for Illustrated Classics, Alexander the Great, and Crispers

"Long is the way and hard, that out of Hell leads up to Light."
                                  —John Milton, *Paradise Lost, Book 2*

"In that outlandish figure they beheld what they envied most and what they most reviled. If their hearts went out to him it was yet true that for very small cause they might also have killed him."
                                  —Cormac McCarthy, *The Crossing*

"It is not flesh and blood, but heart which makes us fathers and sons."

                                  —Friedrich von Schiller

The boy lay under the kitchen table, tucked between an old cardboard box and the wall, hidden from the man who stood at the kitchen door.

The man wiped his hair back from his face. A fine sweat had broken over his brow, and he could feel the warm dampness on the back of his neck as well. He drew a long breath. The boy's foster father had fought hard, then desperately at the end. Considering the corpse, the man felt a slim measure of admiration. Then he stepped over it. The kitchen floor creaked.

From under the table, the boy saw the long tail of the man's coat and his boots as he crossed the room. There was blood on the toe of the right one. A dark shine. There were also smears of blood on the man's right thigh and knee, from where the foster father had slumped against him, but this the boy could not see.

On the stovetop, the frying pan hissed and spat grease. A fetid expulsion of steam. The smell of the hotdogs beginning to burn mixed with the apartment's odour of stale cigarette smoke and the result was sour. Another smell hung over all of it, bodily and rank. Like the grime on the edge of the toilet seat.

A glass bottle of ketchup lay smashed in the middle of the kitchen floor. The boy's foster mother had knocked it from the counter in her haste to defend herself. As the man stepped over the spill, the boy settled his gaze on the thick red paste, thinking it looked like the *real* thing. Not like the dark stuff on the stranger's boot. Not like the stuff that was starting to pool around his foster father's head. But how blood should look. Bright and thick, like on TV.

The boy's foster mother crouched in the corner of the kitchen below the edge of the counter. Her nose was running. The kitchen knife she'd used to cut up the hotdogs was gripped between white knuckles. It's sharp point, gleaming in the fluorescent light, jumped side to side.

The man stopped in front of the woman and looked down at her. His hair fell over his face.

"Where is he?" the man said.

The woman's hands trembled. She said nothing.

"I know he's here somewhere," the man said. "Call him. Tell him to come out."

"I don't know where he is," the woman blurted. "He's hiding. He always just hides. Please . . ."

Before the woman had a chance to say more, the man wrestled the knife from her hands and threw it across the room. It struck the pan from the stove and sent both to the floor in a splash of grease and smoke. The boy heard the clatter and jumped, then hunkered farther back behind the cardboard box.

Looming over the woman, the man yelled, "Where is the boy?"

When she said nothing, he lifted her by the shoulders and struck her across the face. She tottered and he struck her with the back of his hand and she fell to the floor.

"Do you want to end up like *that*?" the man said, gesturing to her dead partner.

"Go to hell," the woman said, her lips bleeding.

Under the table, the boy shut his eyes and tried to think about everything that was happening. He thought hard about his foster mother—*Evie*—picturing her face, and he tried to picture the stranger. He was trying to think about them in his other way, his *special-thinking*. Like he had on nights when his foster father would come home late, yelling and stinking of sweat and beer, and Evie would slam and lock the bathroom door. Sometimes on those nights, if the boy thought about them in his special way, he could make it all stop—

The man grabbed the boy's foster mother by the hair and she screamed. Her feet kicked out, and her heel slid through the ketchup on the floor. She was screaming no, no, no, as he started to drag her from the kitchen.

The boy looked out from behind the box, and for a moment he witnessed his foster mother's face, bright red, with the man's huge hand gripping a fistful of her hair.

Then she was gone, dragged over the body of her dead husband into the front hall. The boy covered his ears but still he could hear her screaming and screaming and then it stopped.

The boy uncovered his ears. He listened. Then he heard the stranger's footsteps again. He was crossing the front hall.

A door crashed open—the bathroom. The boy heard the shower curtain screech along the rod. Then footsteps again, across the hall and back through the kitchen and around the corner into the bedroom. Another door kicked in. A springy piece of furniture flipped and crashed.

The boy sat and listened and he could feel his heartbeat in his ears. He looked out at the feet of his foster father, dirty socks, greasy holes in the heels. He listened again to the noise of the man in the other room. The sound of metal hangers clanged and clothes padded into piles, then the loud crash of a shelf.

The boy crawled out from behind the cardboard box and squatted on the kitchen floor. He waited. His heart raced. He heard nothing in that breath. The other room was quiet.

The boy looked down at his foster father. *Adam.* A man the boy had once tried to call dad. Adam's eyes looked glazed over and empty now, the left was more bloodshot than usual.

There was another sudden crash from the other room and something slammed against the wall with a thud.

The boy sprang over Adam's dead body and into the front hall. He saw Evie slumped against the wall and stopped in front of her. Head hanging over her breast, hair a tangled mess. But unlike Adam, she wasn't empty. She was still alive. The boy's face softened with relief even as tears ran down his face.

Then he was running. Straight to the door.

The man heard the boy in the hall and rushed out from the other room. The boy grasped the doorknob in both hands and turned it. Just as he pulled the door open it slammed shut again, the man's hand pressed flat against it above the boy's head.

The boy looked up. The man loomed massively in his heavy, dark coat.

His long, blackish-brown hair hung over his face to his chin and mixed with the length of his beard. His mouth was small and hidden. Through his hair the boy glimpsed the man's dark grey eyes and a hardened, immovable expression.

They stood, poised one against the other, and then all at once the boy kicked out, aiming for the man's crotch, but his foot skipped off the man's shin. Reflexively, the man grabbed the boy by the neck and hammered him against the door.

The boy shook and squirmed, twisting his head as his face began to redden. His brown eyes widened and he gulped for breath.

The man recalled his instructions not to kill the child, but he couldn't bring himself to let go. He could feel the boy's manic throat contractions against his palm. If he held on much longer he would feel the bones and cartilage start to break, and the blood vessels in the boy's eyes would burst.

And yet he did not relent. Something was happening to the boy's eyes. At first the man thought it was only the eyeballs beginning to hemorrhage, but it was something else. He could *feel* it, and the sight was stirring him to anger. One moment the boy's eyes were brown, the next they had brightened to a light tan, and then, like a spark, the boy's eyes turned the colour of rust. A look of stark defiance flashed across his face.

I know you. . . .

The thought passed through the man's mind like a bullet, and his whole arm tensed with a renewed grip that nearly snapped the boy's neck. What anger stirred in him had sharpened into pure hatred. The boy's rust-coloured eyes bulged, and his face purpled. The man was set to kill him.

And then the boy blinked. All at once, the rusty hue vanished from his irises and they were brown once again. Brown and terrified.

The man saw it and almost gasped with a wave of self-repugnance. He was strangling a child. His anger rebounded and he loosened his grip and dropped the boy to the floor.

CHAPTER TWO

Outside the apartment there was movement and carried voices. The man picked up the boy and took him back into the kitchen and stood him on his feet. The boy was shivering and his legs had little strength and the man had to kneel and hold him by the shoulders for a moment until he could stay up on his own.

"Don't move," the man said.

Then he went out again to the front hall and took the boy's jacket from the hanger and grabbed a pair of boots from the mess on the floor and returned and outfitted the boy. Before zipping up the jacket, he reached in and tore out the two main pockets.

"Stick your hands in," he said.

Without a word the boy put his hands through the now open holes. The man reached under his heavy coat and pulled out a thick black zip tie. He yanked the boy's wrists fully through the holed pockets and lashed them tight together with the tie. Then he pulled the jacket closed in front and drew the zipper up to his chin.

When they were both ready, the man took hold of the boy's shoulders again and said, "Now, you look at me. You're coming with me now. We're leaving this place. Look at me."

The boy looked.

The man said, "You think you see a man when you look at me, but you don't. I'm something much more. I'm faster and stronger than any normal man. If you hurt me, I'll barely feel it. If you knock me down, I'll get right back up. If you run from me, I will always find you. Trust me now when I tell you that I am like no other thing in this world. And if you disobey me, if you even make a move without me telling you to, I'll kill you."

From off the man's hands, the boy could smell Evie's hair, that sweetly soiled scent of an unwashed scalp. It was not altogether unpleasant, and a strange sense of comfort came over him suddenly. It was just as swiftly swept away. The boy stared at the man's hands. A killer's hands. His knuckles looked like jagged stones.

The man said, "When we go out that door you will walk silently. If you make a sound, I'll rip out your tongue. Do you understand?"

The boy stood still, said nothing, but his eyes narrowed.

The man nodded. Then he turned the boy around and led him to the door. They went out quickly and the man closed the door and they started down the hall.

"Hey," called a voice from behind them.

The man glanced over his shoulder. A portly, balding man in a maroon cardigan was standing in the hallway. He was holding a half-eaten chicken leg in his hand. The man kept walking.

"Hey!" the portly man called again. "Hey, I'm talking to you. What was all that noise?"

The man shoved the boy and hurried to the stairwell and banged the door open with his shoulder. He glanced back and saw the portly man standing in front of the apartment door, pulling a string of keys from his belt.

Inside the stairwell, the man picked the boy up by the waist and started down. From above in the hall, a voice shouted, "Oh my god, oh my god!"

In the foyer, the man set the boy down again and gripped him hard by the shoulder, his fingers digging into the boy's collarbone.

They walked past the elevators to the front doors. The elevator was ticking down as they stepped out onto the street.

Within the sudden darkness of night the man drew a cool breath. It was snowing lightly. Twinkling in streetlights that glowed above a shadowed city.

Right away the man saw *them*. Two dark figures lurking across the street.

Whoever or whatever they were was beyond his knowing. They seemed hardly more than shadows. But he could feel them calling the night, calling to him as well, like a steady sucking in of breath. And most of all he could see their eyes, shimmering like mirrors in the dark.

When they looked his way, the man saw it clear as day: the night was drawn to them, but it rebounded when it touched their eyes, perhaps met with its own making, an unnatural glow that betrayed them even as they tried to hide within it.

They stood perfectly still, but their timidity, or their patience, would last only so long. The man could sense it. They were like wolves.

The man looked down the street to his car. There he saw the gleam of more eyes. There were two others standing at the mouth of an alleyway.

Four on one.

If they rushed him, they would have a fair chance of seizing the boy.

The man started for his car, then paused and stepped back. His driver side door was ajar, just barely noticeable. He could tell the front hood had been opened as well.

He drew a very long breath then, realizing he wouldn't be getting away as fast as he'd hoped. The two sets of eyes in the alleyway watched him steadily.

If they wanted a fight, fine, he would give them one. They weren't the only ones who could call the night.

He looked up into the sky, searching above the glow of city lights to the darkest patch he could find. He felt his body begin to hum as the darkness within him sent out its call. It's summoning. And then the night came to him. It rushed down like the charge of some great and ancient animal. The man held his breath for the shortest of moments in awe. The sense it gave him was always extraordinary, the overwhelming impression of companionship. A home bidding him welcome.

Then, like he'd injected burning gasoline into his veins, he felt his heart slam in his chest. His spine curved back, and the hairs on the back of his neck stood up. He squared his shoulders and glared across the street at the others.

"Come on and rush me," he said under his breath. "Come on, try it."

He wondered which of them he would kill first. The spirit of the night was running quick in him now, and he was actually excited to get his hands on them. It had been a long time since he had called to the night, and he'd almost forgotten what it felt like. The immense strength of its company, like a mob, and the violent persuasion of its voice. He would grab the first that came at him and tear out its heart. But he would still have to be quick. Four on one were not odds he liked.

At that moment, blue lights shone through the snow from down the street. With a slight wave of relief, the man saw a bus coming. He might not have to fight after all. He hurried to the stop at the corner, dragging the boy with him. The others across the street moved as well. From the corner of his eye, the man saw them shifting out from their shadows. He readied himself.

But before anything could happen, the bus drew up and stopped and the man got on quickly with the boy. He dropped a handful of change in the fare box and moved to the back. As the bus pulled away, the man looked out the window and saw the four of *them* gathered in the street near his car, their eyes darkly aglow. They hadn't wanted a fight; they wanted the boy. He wondered when he would meet them again.

The boy sat in a double seat and the man stood beside it, his hand on the rail and his other hand near the boy. The boy stared down at his feet. Underneath his jacket he twisted his wrists against the ties. The man looked straight ahead, his expression stern and pensive.

We're heading east. Get to the subway. Go south.

The bus stopped at a red light and the engine hummed. The man looked out the window again and from afar he heard sirens. They were ringing, louder and louder.

The man turned and faced the red glare of the traffic light, the colour bleeding across the front windshield. The night was ebbing from him. He could see his own obscured reflection in the glass, and he realized he was not holding the boy. He placed his hand on the boy's shoulder and felt the boy flinch. The light turned green. The bus drove. The man closed his eyes.

The boy sat very still now. He listened to the sound of the sirens and he wished they would grow louder instead of fade away. Only once did he dare look up, and when he did, he saw the man's eyes closed, his expression forlorn with a deep crease through his brow. The boy opened his mouth at the man's face as if screaming as loud as he could, but then shut it and looked away.

The bus made several stops and then arrived at the station. When the doors opened, the man hauled the boy to his feet.

"Come on," he said.

They went down the escalator to the southbound subway platform. The man led the boy along to a space well away from everyone else and then stopped and held the boy back against the wall.

The boy hung his head. He stared down at the man's boots, and he could smell blood. The thought of running hit him, but he stayed still, fear burying the idea. He wished the wall would open up behind him so he could fall through it and get away.

When the train came, they got on and sat at the back of the car near the doors. They said nothing and no one spoke to them and the boy stared at his lap the entire time. His wrists were hurting.

The train announced that they had arrived at Queen's Park Station.

"Let's go," the man said.

They came up out of the subway and the man looked around under the traffic lights and the falling snow, but he saw no one waiting for them. He led the boy west along College Street at a brisk pace.

At the corner of Spadina Avenue, the man stopped and held the boy tight against him with his huge hand on the boy's chest, considering his choices.

He watched the traffic lights and the wet sloshing procession of cars and the street trolleys full of passengers gliding through the slush, all of it a glaring collage of possibility and indecision. Against his palm, he felt the boy's heartbeat, a strong and even pace. For a moment it felt almost doubled. Then the man realized the boy was shivering. He made a decision.

When the lights changed, the man led the boy across the street and walked up to the Maverick Hotel and went in and requested a room.

The concierge had thin blond hair, wire-framed glasses. He had a sore on his bottom lip. He peered from behind the counter with a languid expression, glancing from the man to the boy and back to the man.

"Rate's forty an hour or sixty-five for the night," he said.

The man paid for the night and waited.

"Room 408," the concierge said, procuring a key card from under the counter. "Just try not to make too much of a mess."

The man grabbed the key card, almost before the concierge noticed he'd reached for it, and led the boy across the foyer. He took one look at the elevator, its faded chrome doors riddled with dents, and hurried past to the stairwell.

The concierge watched them until they were out of sight. The stairwell door shut with a soft click.

The concierge rolled his eyes. "Fucking perverts," he grumbled.

On the fourth floor, the man shoved the boy along the hall to the room and pushed him inside after the key card beeped. He stepped in and flipped on the light, closed the door, bolted it, and fastened the chain. When he turned around, he saw the boy huddled in the far corner of the room, his head bowed against his knees.

It was a small plain room. A sagging double bed, telephone on the nightstand, television on a stout grey bureau against the wall. The man went and stood near the boy, looking out the window to the street. He watched the crowd gathered at the streetcar stop. Mostly downturned heads. Regular people in jackets and toques. As he watched, there was one person who looked up towards him, but their face was in shadow, their eyes plain and unbetraying, and they looked away almost immediately. He nodded and pulled the dingy yellow curtains closed.

He turned to the boy, who was still huddled in the corner, eyes averted, silent.

All the better for now.

The man shook off his jacket and tossed it onto the bed, causing the lime green cover to shift and reveal the stained sheets underneath. He noticed, then, all the stains on the carpeting, the grease and dust on the darkened television screen, the discolouring of the worn telephone, a fist-sized hole in the wall. It filled him with a sudden revulsion and dismay not only for the room and the world outside but his own place in it as well. Drawing a deep breath, he went into the bathroom and splashed some water on his face, scratching his cheeks and chin thoroughly through his beard. He avoided looking in the mirror. He turned off the taps. Before he left, he pulled the shower curtain back.

He came out into the main room, regarding the space again, then ducked down and lifted the bed-skirt. He stood again and nodded.

He looked at the boy. Still huddled, still silent.

The man walked around the bed to the nightstand and considered the telephone. The stain on the receiver marked the passage of countless callers, the grip of many sweaty hands, the crook of unwashed necks. He lifted the receiver to his ear, adding his own mark to the phone's history, and dialled the only number he knew. He waited while it rang, his shoulders hunched, looking at the floor. When the call was answered, he straightened.

"August," he said. "Sorry to wake you."

The boy looked up. He saw that the man's back was turned and so he sat and watched him. He was too far away to hear the other voice on the phone, but he wanted to watch. For some reason it made him feel less afraid. It was just a man talking on the telephone.

The man said, "Listen, I'll be visiting . . . tomorrow some time . . . I'll need to borrow your truck. Yes. No, I'm all right."

The man glanced over his shoulder at the boy, who looked quickly at his knees.

"A boy," the man said. "I don't know, six or seven, it doesn't matter. I made a deal, August. A fair deal. If they hold up their end, I'll hold up mine." The man was quiet. He was listening. When he spoke again there was heat in his voice. He said, "I didn't call you for a lecture. Like I said, I'll be visiting tomorrow. Don't make any plans. Good night."

The man hung up and looked over his shoulder. The boy had moved.

He was sitting on the foot of the bed with his eyes open wide, a blue light flashing across his face. The man turned and saw the bright television. It was set to a news station. The anchor's mouth moved mutely. The boy looked up at the man and did not speak but looked at him straight and then wiggled his arms from inside the jacket.

"No," the man said. "But it's good to know you're listening."

The man grabbed the television remote from the side table and switched on the volume.

"A six-year-old boy is missing after a gruesome home invasion near St. Clair and Vaughan Road. Officials are not releasing names at this time. One suspect is reported. Adult male, forty to fifty years of age, tall, dark hair, beard, seen leaving the area with suspected kidnapping victim."

The bulletin cut to an interview with the building's superintendent, the portly man who had stopped them in the hall. *"Ya, oh, he was huge! Easily the biggest man I've ever seen. I saw him leaving with the kid, and I tried to stop him but he pulled a gun on me."*

The newscaster returned. *"Police are asking anyone with information to contact the tip line at the bottom of your screen."*

The man shook his head. "Looks like we'll be leaving sooner than later," he said, turning off the television

The boy looked up at him, tight-lipped, and wiggled his arms again. The man made a face, as if a small part of him was considering it, but before he could speak there was a knock at the door.

CHAPTER THREE

The knock came again, and the man stepped towards the door. From behind him he heard the mattress's old springs twang loudly. He turned and saw the boy had jumped up from the bed, ready on his feet.

The man glared at him. He could see the intensity in the boy's face, his little brown eyes trained on the door, as if each knock was the tolling of some salvation bell. There was a new feeling in the room like static in the air. A tense, hopeful energy of escape.

"Get in the corner," the man said.

The boy stood still. He glanced once at the man and then returned his attention to the door. It was the police, he reasoned. The guy at the front desk must have called them. It had to be.

The man raised his fist, and the boy's eye followed it. His nerve wavered.

"Into the corner," the man said. "Now."

The boy obeyed and went into the corner of the room. The man followed him.

"Sit," he said.

The boy sat. The man steadied himself at the window. He tore aside the yellow curtain and glanced out to the street. No police cruisers. No flashing lights.

Another knock.

The man swept his hair from his face and turned to the boy.

"Lie down and put your face to the ground," he said.

The boy hesitated, but then obeyed. The man walked to the door, unfastened the locks, unbolted and opened it.

The hallway was empty.

The man leaned out and peered down the hall in both directions. Nothing. It appeared that the door to the stairwell at the end of the hall was slightly open, but that might easily have been his own doing earlier. A television chattered from one of the rooms, the low roar of canned laughter. Otherwise, the hallway was deathly quiet.

He stepped back into the room and locked the door, refastening the chain. When he turned around, he saw the visitor standing in the centre of the room between the bed and the window.

The man froze, but only for a moment before he recognized the visitor. His silver hair, his clean white suit. He went by the name Gabriel.

"I trust we are still in accord?" Gabriel said. His voice was loud and it lingered in the small room.

The man nodded.

"Good." Gabriel glanced down at the boy "We like to keep a watchful eye on our interests."

"Is that all?" the man said.

Gabriel formed a pyramid with his hands in front of his chest. He looked at the man and grinned and his jaw looked huge, as if the majority of his personage resided in his mouth. "I have come to ensure you continue in accordance with your oath," he said. "You have procured the child as was agreed. I trust you have no hesitations regarding what comes next. It is imperative that the child reaches the church alive. There we will meet the Adversary."

"Who's your Adversary?"

"*The* Adversary. There is only one." Then he said, "Occupy yourself with the task at hand and bring the child to the church."

"I know the terms of my oath."

"Very good. Then we have nothing more to discuss."

"Why don't you take him?" asked the man. "I still don't see what reason you have for involving me in this."

"It is not our way to engage physically. We are mere influencers. You, however, are a creature of action. Does it matter so much why you help us, as long as we help you in return? You do still want your reward, do you not?"

The man's face tightened, as if the mention of his reward caused him pain.

Gabriel said, "You do still wish to see your sweet Allison again? To hear her voice? To hold her in your—"

"Yes," the man said, looking at the floor.

"Then you must fulfill your oath. There is absolutely no profit in becoming an oath breaker, I assure you."

"What will you do with him?" the man asked.

Gabriel only grinned. His white teeth flashed in the yellow light of the room. Then his mouth closed and smoothed.

While they had been talking, the boy had been listening. His right ear was pressed against the carpet, but he had heard enough to think again about rescue. Slowly, he turned his head to the side to look up.

He saw his captor standing in front of the door, and he saw the back of the other man. The visitor's white suit looked so clean. His white leather shoes were spotless.

He thought maybe the visitor was a lawyer or someone from social services. Maybe they had come to get him. They had come and taken him from bad places before. Maybe the hotel guy had called them instead of the police, and they were here to take him back to the Centre. Maybe he would get to live with the other kids again for a while.

The boy was thinking like this when all at once a cold shiver ran down his spine and settled in his stomach. If he had had a tail, he would have tucked it between his legs.

The visitor looked odd, the boy now thought, his fresh white suit was too white. His back and shoulders were extremely stiff and rigid. As if his fine clothes were all the wrong fit or his body as a whole was a source of discomfort. Looking at him, the strangest feeling of an old dream, the memory of a dream, washed over the boy. He felt somehow that he knew the visitor, but the familiarity was matched with a sense of danger.

This person is not your friend.

The thought made the boy numb, and he closed his eyes.

"Bring the child to the church," Gabriel said. "I will come again, then."

"There were others," the man said. "When I grabbed the kid, there were others who could draw the night like I do. They seemed young, just fledglings, their eyes gave them away. But they were waiting for us. Did you offer *them* a reward, too?"

"We came to you and you alone because we believe you can keep the child alive and ensure that our interests are upheld. But your search for the child has been felt *widely*. Many know that you have found him. And they are coming."

The man's expression was knowing. "If the fledglings found me once, they'll find me again. And chances are there will be Michaelian Knights not far behind them. This is going to be a long night."

"Do whatever you must. As I said before, we are mere influencers in this place. We will not be able to help you. You understand you are on your own?"

"It's the only thing I've ever understood."

At that moment, there was a rubbery thud against the window. The man and the visitor turned and watched as a pair of legs dangled outside, feeling for a foothold. They steadied on the ledge. Then one foot swung away and came forward again, smashing hard into the glass with a loud crack.

"Well," said the visitor. "Here they come now."

Even before the visitor had finished speaking, the man ran to the boy and lifted him up under his arm.

A booted foot came through the window, the glass shattering onto the carpet, but the man was already away. He thought to carry the boy out into the hall, get back out onto the street, but as he reached the door he heard running in the hall. Gabriel was gone, but someone else was coming their way, fast. The man spun and went into the bathroom.

He set the boy down inside the tub and hurried back out, pulling the door shut after him.

In the main room he found the fledglings waiting for him.

He knew right away it was the same four he had escaped from in the street. The calling of the night connected them with a strange intimacy, as if they already knew each other's names. Standing now in the yellow light of the hotel room, he saw them stripped of their shadowy menace. They looked like a band of rock-and-rollers, the man thought, cut straight out of a magazine, two guys and two girls. He half expected them to be holding electric guitars and drumsticks, but instead they held short curved knives. They spread into the centre of the room in a semicircle. The closest one squared his shoulders, holding his knife out in front of him.

"We've come for the heart, old one," he said. "We know you found it. Just give it over. We have no fight with you."

"You've been tracking me," the man said.

"Your name is old and your movements through the night are easy to follow. We want the heart."

"The heart of a child."

"It's not a child. If we eat the heart, we will become as the Lord. We will be free of this place."

The man stepped towards them and the young man flinched, then steadied his knife.

The man said, "What if I say no?"

"There are four of us."

The man could tell they were about to strike. If they all got on him at once, he would be in trouble. He knew he needed to break them of their pack mentality, set an example with one and the others would fall apart.

He locked eyes with the young man holding the knife and said, "No."

When the knife came at him, he ducked and sidestepped and came up behind his attacker, grabbing the back of his head with one hand like it was a piece of fruit. His other hand went to the young man's mouth, his fingers going down his throat, and then he pulled down hard and there was a loud crack as he tore off the lower jaw. With a choked wail, a gush of phlegm and blood spewed over the man's hand and the young man dropped to the floor.

The three others stood in a row together and their eyes and mouths were wide with horror. The man was panting as he wiped blood from his face and swept his hair back and gazed at them with eyes rounded black. Then he stepped towards them.

Inside the bathroom, the boy sat in the tub. He wriggled his arms out from the bottom of his jacket and raised his wrists to his mouth and started biting at the zip tie. The plastic was strong and it hurt his teeth, but he twisted his wrists to the right and chewed with his incisors. He was panting from the strain, his breath warm on his wrists, and he could taste blood in his mouth. Either cut by the tie or biting his own skin, he could not tell. He was hurting, and his breath was becoming hot. Really hot. He bit down hard and felt the plastic soften. Steam rose past his eyes. He bit again. The plastic felt like a soft eraser between his teeth, and then the zip tie snapped off. It landed between his feet in the tub. The broken ends looked like they had been melted. He pulled his arms out from the torn pockets of his jacket and rubbed his wrists, careful not to touch where they were bleeding.

At that moment, the bathroom door was hit hard and the boy sat up, eyes wide. A series of loud thuds and bangs rolled across the wall and ended with a hard crash. The boy listened to the progress of the noise, trembling and holding his breath. He felt dazed and weak.

A heavy slam against the floor in the other room shook the bathroom mirror. Fast footsteps crossed the room and then there was a loud crash of glass and breaking parts. The boy pictured the television hitting the floor.

Slowly, the boy crawled out of the tub and squatted in the middle of the bathroom facing the door. The sounds from the other room had mostly stopped.

The boy waited. His hands were balled into fists, but they felt small. He looked around the room for anything he might use. Finally he found an old, dirty toilet brush wedged behind the column of the sink. He pulled it out but it felt light and even more useless than his own fists. There was nothing else.

He placed the brush on the floor and stepped on the bristled end and pulled the handle back over the edge of his foot and it bent and then the old plastic snapped. He looked at it. The plastic was dull. But he held onto it. Maybe he could use it to jab the man in the eye, he thought. He lifted the hem of his jacket and tucked the broken handle into the front of his pants.

The bathroom door was pulled open, and the man entered. He breathed in big huffs and his clothes were wet and glistening in the parted light. His face was drenched in blood, particularly around his mouth and dripping from his beard. The boy moved away until the backs of his knees were touching the edge of the tub.

The man turned on the taps in the sink and ran them hot, then splashed his face over and over and scrubbed with his nails at his beard to break up the already drying clots of blood. While he washed, he looked sideways at the boy.

"How in hell did you get your hands free?"

The boy said nothing. He could smell the tang of blood and that other sick scent that was almost sweet that he was learning was called death.

The man splashed his face one final time and turned off the taps. He wiped his hair back. Lines of water ran down his face and drops sprinkled in his beard.

"What's that in the front of your pants?" he asked.

The boy fidgeted. His face burned. Caught, he was terrified.

"Give it to me," the man said.

The boy lifted the front of his jacket and pulled the broken brush handle from his pants and placed it in the man's palm.

The man studied it. "Were you planning to stick me with it?"

Still, the boy said nothing. The man scrutinized the useless weapon, the cheap quality of the plastic, and then he broke the brush in two and tossed the duller end onto the floor.

He held the sharper piece of the broken handle out in front of the boy. The tip was now raggedly pointed. It was a decent shiv.

"Now listen to me," the man said. "I'm not going to tie you up again. I need you to trust me now. There is nothing for you to go back to, so there's no point in running from me. I'm the only one who can protect you."

"Protect me?" the boy asked.

"There are people out there who want something from you. I don't know how many, but there will be more."

"Are they *mean* people?"

"Yes, they are mean people. Very mean."

The boy nodded earnestly and it seemed he understood about *mean people*.

The man wagged the shiv in the air and said, "If they catch us again, you might have to use this. Here. Take it. Put it in your pocket and be ready to use it."

Slowly, the boy reached out and took the homemade shiv from the man. He held it tightly and examined the new pointed end and touched it with the tip of his finger. It was sharp. He put it in his pants pocket.

"We have to go," the man said. "It's not safe here anymore."

"Evan," the boy said.

The man stopped.

The boy was looking up at him. He said, "My name is Evan."

"Okay."

"Now you have to tell me your name."

The man stared at the boy. Then he sighed and said, "I'm Rook."

"Rook? What kind of name is Rook?"

"My kind. Now let's go."

They went through the main room, and Rook stepped over the wreckage of bodies and furniture. Evan stopped and stared. There was blood everywhere.

Rook nudged him towards the door and then stepped back and pulled from under the overturned mattress his heavy coat, swinging his arms into the sleeves. Snow blew in through the smashed window and the sound of sirens carried. They went out.

Chapter Four

When they came down to the first floor, Rook stopped Evan at the stairwell door and looked into the foyer.

"Damn," he muttered.

Dark blue uniforms. Holstered pistols.

There were two police officers questioning the concierge. Rook listened through the door.

". . . So you said there *was* a man that came in here, and he had a kid with him?" said the taller of the two officers.

"Yeah, there was a guy like that," the concierge said. "A lot of people come in and out of here. There was a group of punks that came through a bit, looked around and left."

"They were looking for the man as well?"

"How the hell should I know," the concierge said. "They walked in, looked around a bit, and walked back out. Some people are just curious what goes on in here. Christ, if these walls could talk."

One of the police officers stepped back and removed his peaked cap. "Listen, we need to know what room the man and the boy are staying in. Are they still here?"

"I can't tell you that. Client confidentiality."

"Look you greasy rat-fuck, the only thing that's going to be confidential is how many bones we're going to break if you don't cooperate."

"You just try it. I got cameras in here. You just try it."

The other officer put his arm in front of his partner. "The man is wanted for murder," he said.

Rook stepped away from the door. He was surprised that the police had found them already. After the fledglings, he had expected to be tracked by a special investigations unit of Michaelian Knights—witch hunters, as August called them. Given their absence, Rook was not unpleased with the situation.

Down the hall there was a solid grey door with a horizontal push-release bar. A fading orange sign above read: *Exit*.

Rook glanced once more into the foyer and saw the taller officer walking out to the street. The other remained at the desk. He took Evan's hand and led him down the hall to the door. Pushing the release bar, Rook shouldered the door open into the night.

A blast of cold wind pulled the door fully open and it swung back against the side of the building with a hard bang. Evan shivered. The police officer standing watch over the side exit stopped short with a stick of chewing gum halfway in his mouth. His face and hands were red from the cold. Rook saw him and saw only him. For a moment they were all of them completely still. Then the officer dropped the gum and reached for his pistol.

Rook pushed Evan aside and the boy fell into a mound of snow along the side of the building. The cop's handgun was halfway out of his holster, but Rook moved much faster. He crouched low and rolled, springing to his feet at the officer's elbow.

Evan heard the policeman's panicked shout over the wind and it sounded fake and faraway like they were in a movie. Evan was looking at his hands, wiping the snow from them. Then he heard another cry and a bright flash lit up the night and he jumped at the gunshot.

In the afterglow of the shot, Evan saw the officer gripping his right arm and a wave of terror went through him. The officer's arm was snapped backwards at the elbow, the white bone splintering out from his jacket sleeve. His pistol dangled from his trembling hand, caught on numb fingers.

As Evan watched, Rook gripped the policeman's shoulder and struck him hard on the side of the neck, and the officer crumpled to the ground.

Rook rushed back over to Evan and reached out his hand.

Evan recoiled. All his earlier fear returned and he saw Rook as a hulking monster. A killer. He scrambled along the side of the building towards the open door.

"What are you doing?" Rook said. "I'm not going to hurt you."

But Evan was beyond listening. He clambered to his feet and dashed inside the building, out of the cold and the dark and into the hall, starting to cry as he ran.

In his head, he heard the gunshot again, saw the officer's backwards elbow. He saw the bodies strewn across the hotel room. He saw his foster parents lying beaten.

The wind roared behind him and everything was loud and terrible and unending. His mouth was open to scream but nothing came out. His breath was trapped in his stomach.

Three more cops rushed down the corridor from the foyer towards him. The first stopped and grabbed Evan, while the other two continued past. Evan looked into the woman's face, but could not hear what she was saying. His mind was back in another room, hiding in the closet.

The officer lifted Evan into her arms and started back to the foyer. Over her shoulder, Evan looked down the corridor to the exit. The two other cops had gone out. The doorway was empty. A snow-swept space where Rook had been, as if the wind had blown him away or he'd never been there at all. Evan continued to stare down the hall, into the night, with a vacant look on his face. Fresh tears ran down his cheeks.

Then he was moving away, bouncing against the officer's shoulder.

The officer carried him into the foyer and set him down in one of the lobby chairs. There were cops coming and going through the front doors, and the one that had carried him stood by his side. After a moment, a woman with blonde hair joined them and she knelt before Evan and dabbed at his tears with a tissue. Evan considered her and thought she looked nothing like Evie. Where was Evie, he wondered.

Evie was dead. No, she wasn't dead. He hadn't killed Evie.

The blonde woman started asking him questions.

Evan watched her mouth open and close. But he said nothing and sat very still. He looked down at his hands. Someone wrapped a blanket around Evan's shoulders.

The woman left for a moment and spoke with another policeman and returned. She squatted in front of Evan and curled the front lock of her hair behind her ear and resumed her questioning. Evan's ears started ringing. He heard a dull hum. Then—

"Can you tell me anything about the man who took you?" the woman asked. "Anything he said? Anything that might help us find him? Did he say where he was taking you?"

Evan said nothing.

•

After some time, two officers escorted Evan outside to a police cruiser. It was still snowing and it shimmered in the blue and red lights. Evan could see his breath. He looked up once past all the lights and the gathering crowd and for a moment he thought he saw Rook watching him, but it was only two, tall men in dark coats standing close together. He looked down at his feet. The police officers opened the back door of the cruiser and gestured for Evan to climb inside.

Just as the boy was stepping from the curb, the two men he'd mistaken for Rook approached the car. Tall men, they both wore black wool peacoats with the collars turned up over their chins, and their hair was dark and neatly combed. They stopped short of the car and addressed the two cops.

"Evening," one of the two men said. His face was long and grey.

"Keep it back," said the officers.

The grey-faced man reached inside the breast of his jacket and retrieved a leather-encased badge. "Special Investigations," he said. "I'm Agent Clarke. This is Agent Gallo."

The second man reached inside his jacket and presented his own badge.

"Special Investigations, eh," said one of the officers, studying the badges. "Are you with the RCMP?"

Agent Clarke replaced his badge and said, "We're not at liberty to say."

At the edge of the police cordon, curious faces gawked. Cell phones flashed above their human sightlines. From somewhere a cop shouted, "Come on, keep it moving. Nothing to see here."

Agent Gallo reached for Evan and said, "We'll take the boy from here."

"Hang on," the officer in front of him started. "This kid's part of a homicide investigation, you can't just—"

"Believe me, we can," Clarke said. "This is much more serious. This child is a key witness in the investigation of a known domestic terrorist."

"Domestic terrorist? Oh give me a break. This is some Ottawa bullshit."

"We're sorry for the inconvenience, here, officers."

"This is just . . ."

Clarke said, "Think of it this way. You've done your part in this.

It's all one big process, and we're all on the same team. You found the boy. Now it's our turn."

Agent Gallo reached past the two officers and took Evan gently by the arm. The officers hung back, shaking their heads.

"Don't you worry," Gallo whispered to Evan. "You're more than safe with us."

Evan went along easily with the Special Investigations agents. Their hands were flat and gentle on his back. He glanced once more through the shimmer of snow and lights, but he saw nothing of Rook or any of the others.

Gallo helped Evan climb into the backseat of their black SUV and closed the door. Inside, the seat was stiff and cold and smelled of the leather upholstery. The agents had not bothered to secure Evan's seatbelt and he slid around freely. He felt light and he wanted to laugh. His breath came in a gulp that he held in his mouth before letting it out.

It's over, he thought. *I'm free.*

Evan looked at the dashboard as Clarke and Gallo climbed into the front seats. A small, silver cross hung from the rear-view mirror. The doors locked with a loud click. Agent Clarke started the engine and slid the transmission into drive and pulled away from the curb.

As they reached the intersection, the traffic light turned yellow. Clarke laid his foot onto the gas pedal and the SUV sped through the light, turning sharply left, and Evan slid across the seat. The shrill crying of car horns erupted behind them.

CHAPTER FIVE

They drove through the city in silence. Evan sat in the backseat and watched the windows shimmer and shift with electric lights, blurring green and red on the glass. He was feeling better. The car was warm. He fiddled with his fingers and filled his cheeks with air, letting his breath escape through puckered lips.

They crossed a bridge and Evan saw railway cars and tracks covered with snow in the dark below. He slid to the other window and stared up at the CN Tower. He had never been nearer to it and the structure's colossal impression made him feel truly small. He squeezed his fingertips, needing to hold onto something. But the tower's round pinnacle, glowing purple, dazzled him. He smiled. Watching the playful lights, he forgot about the dark city and all the bad that was behind him. He felt good and safe, charmed by what seemed like magic.

They went down a low hill and the CN Tower was lost to view behind rows of glass-walled skyscrapers. Then they turned and the engine revved and sped up, joining other cars zipping past the windows, and Evan heard the whoosh of each car as the white lights came up and shone straight at them and then away. He looked back to once more see the lights of the city.

A ringing sounded in the car, and Evan spun with a start. In the passenger seat, Agent Gallo shifted and took his phone out. It rang even louder. Ring-ring-ring. It reminded Evan of living at the Centre, when the phones would ring in the night, after hours. The memory gave him a shiver.

Agent Gallo looked at the phone's bright screen and groaned, and then looked at his partner.

"It's Maria," he said.

Clarke glanced at his partner. "Okay, answer it," he said.

Gallo brought the phone to his ear. "Hello, Maria."

Evan could hear the woman's voice, faintly.

"I'm so sorry, Mr. Gallo, but she won't go to sleep. . . . Wants to talk to you. . . . Sorry, Mr. Gallo."

"It's all right, Maria. Put her on."

"Of course, Mr. Gallo. . . . Then she'll go right to sleep. . . . Here she is. . . ."

Evan slid forward to the edge of the seat to listen. A car whooshed past the window as they changed lanes. From out of the phone came a small, soft voice.

"Daddy?"

"Hi, ladybug," Gallo said. "You can't sleep?"

"No, Daddy, I want you to come home."

"Daddy's working, right now, sweetheart. It's late."

"I'm scared, Daddy. . . . There's something outside my window. It's scratching."

"That's just the wind in the trees, sweetie."

"I want you to come home, Daddy."

"Hush now. I'll make you a promise, okay? I promise that when you wake up in the morning, I'll be right there beside you. But first you have to go to sleep."

"You promise?"

"I cross my heart and hope to die. Now go to sleep. I love you."

"I love you, too, Daddy."

"Put Maria back on. . . . Hello, Maria? Let her know I'll be home in the morning. No, it's no bother. Have a good night."

Gallo put the phone away and sat straight and sighed. Clarke looked askance at him but whatever he thought, he said nothing. Evan watched them both, expecting one or the other to speak. After a while he slid back on the wide, leather seat. The car hummed warmly. He closed his eyes.

Soon, he was asleep.

• — •

When Evan woke up, they had exited the highway and were driving at a snail's pace down a dark and narrow road. He sat up and rubbed his eyes. Out the window, the city skyline was far away, like tiny sticks of light in the distance. For a moment, the man Rook came to mind. A dark imagining of him running through the whirling snow and disappearing into the night. Evan was very glad to be away from all of that.

The SUV bumped along the road, turned right and continued over some heavily uneven ground. They were driving among trees and there were no lights save for the moon. Evan put his nose to the window and his breath fogged the glass. He wiped the fog away, and beyond the window he saw the vast rolling of the lake.

They drove for a while longer and then turned again and the headlights shone out over the water when they stopped. Clarke shut off the engine.

"Where are we?" Evan asked, yawning.

Agent Gallo glanced over his shoulder but said nothing, while Agent Clarke opened his door and stepped out. Evan watched Clarke hurry past his window to the back of the SUV. He pulled his legs up and hugged his knees. Still in the passenger seat, Agent

Gallo sat very still, his chin bowed, as if staring with great intent at his kneecaps. The car was draining of warmth.

Then Evan heard the trunk unlock behind him and the pneumatic hum as the door lifted. He looked back through the small space between the seats. In the open cargo area, Clarke was bent over a large black duffle bag. Evan heard the long zipper pull. Over Clarke's arched back, the night was pitch black and the many trees stood bare, with an icy wind blowing through them. Evan could hear the slow ebb and flow of the lake not far away.

At that moment, the door to the back seat unlocked and opened. The cold flooded in. Evan had failed to notice Agent Gallo get out of the car. When he turned, he saw the man standing at the open door with a gun in his hand.

Evan stared at it—a big silver revolver. It was bigger and older looking than the cops' guns. It seemed heavier.

"Get out," Gallo said.

Evan sat still. His eyes fixed on the gun. His heart was starting to race. After a moment, Gallo reached in across the seat and grabbed Evan by the arm and dragged him out. Evan fell and landed on cold, uneven ground, and his fingers went through the snow. There was hard sand underneath. Gallo yanked him to his feet and shut the door.

A beam of light flashed out from the back of the SUV and the trunk door began to close. Agent Clarke came around the side. Evan looked at him and thought for a second that he was someone else entirely. Clarke had changed his clothes. Instead of his peacoat, he wore a long white robe with a green and silver V-shaped sash draped over his shoulders. He carried the flashlight in one hand and clasped a leather-bound book to his chest in the other. Evan saw the glint of a silver cross hanging from Clarke's neck overtop the green of the sash.

"Are you a priest?" Evan asked.

"Silence," Gallo hissed.

"We are Novitiates," Clarke said. "Of the Order of Michaelian Knights."

Evan was about to ask what "novitiates" meant, when the barrel of Gallo's big revolver levelled in front of his face and his mouth went dry. The SUV's automatic locking clicked and then beeped.

"Let's go," Clarke said.

In single file, they walked from the SUV among the trees towards the water's edge. The ground was hard and cratered and covered with snow. Evan could sense the barrel of the gun aimed at the back of his head. The water grew louder as they came out onto the beach. A steady rolling of the waves.

Near the head of the beach, Clarke shone the flashlight over the ground.

"All right," he said. "Here, this is a fitting spot."

They stopped and the two men stood on either side of the boy. Evan put his hand into his pants pocket, feeling for the shiv.

Clarke opened the leather-bound book, holding the flashlight over the pages. He cleared his throat, as if it were crucial that he speak well and be heard. Gallo kept the revolver trained at Evan's head.

Trying to move as little as possible, Evan squeezed his hand around the shiv in his pocket, his fingers cold and sweating. He didn't know what he was going to do or when, but just holding the shiv was something.

From somewhere beyond the glow of the flashlight, in the dark of the trees, they all heard the loud snap of a tree branch. The two Novitiates looked out into the gloom of the trees. Gallo's shoulders lifted as he scanned the perimeter. He thought he saw something move, something more than the shift of shadows and moonlight, but it happened only the once.

"Let's hurry up," Gallo said.

"It can't be rushed," Clarke said. "Every part must be observed in whole. You remember Father Harris's instruction."

"I know. I just mean, let's start already."

"Lead us in prayer."

Gallo drew the sign of the cross in the air and said, "Saint Michael the Archangel, defend us in battle. Be our protection against the wickedness and snares of the devil; may God rebuke him, we humbly pray; and do thou, O Prince of the Heavenly Host, by the power of God, thrust into hell Satan and all evil spirits who wander through the world for the ruin of souls. Amen."

"Amen," Clarke said and nodded. Then he steadied the flashlight over the chosen page and began to read aloud: "And I stood upon the sand—"

Right then, there came a fast whistling from out of the trees across the beach and Agent Clarke gave a cry and the book flew from his hands. The flashlight hit the ground and rolled and the beachhead went into darkness. When the light levelled, it shone flat across the snow and revealed Clarke on his knees. His hands were raised to his chest where he'd been skewered through with a gnawed and broken branch. After a moment of hopeless consideration, Clarke sputtered blood and toppled over.

Quickly, Gallo grabbed Evan and stuck the gun to his head and turned towards the shadowed trees. Evan shut his eyes with the cold steel barrel at his temple. The thoughts that came to him in that moment were not of forgiveness or mercy or God, but instead, for some reason, he was thinking of Gallo's little girl. The phone call from inside the car replayed inside Evan's head.

He's a dad, Evan thought. *He loves his little girl. How can someone who loves with their heart also kill with their hands?*

"I'll kill him," Gallo shouted. "I swear I will!"

Rook walked out of the trees. His heavy coat was open and his hands were empty and he stood out plain in the moonlight. Even against the surrounding night his eyes were a deep voided black. When Evan saw Rook, his heart leapt in his chest. Whether from hope or dread he didn't know. Agent Gallo dug the barrel of the gun against his temple, and Evan whimpered. He could feel Gallo's hand trembling.

"Let the child go and you can live," Rook said.

"No. No, he must die. It has been decreed. I had my doubts before, but I know now that it's true. It's all true. And he must die."

"I won't tell you again. Let him go."

"I have the power of God on my side. You can't frighten me."

"On the contrary, priest. I've frightened you your entire life."

Gallo's face was awash in a cold sweat and his chest and arms trembled. His legs were shaking. And yet he held the boy and the gun with the remnant strength of his conviction.

At that moment, out of the dark of his peripheral vision, Gallo glimpsed a small figure sweep across the beach in the moonlight. He started, swinging his whole body around to face it and pulling the boy with him.

Rook saw it also and he turned.

A wisp of cloth. A pink, spotted nightgown. Tiny footprints tiptoeing across the snow-covered beach. The waves rolled upon the shore and with them carried the little girl's voice.

Daddy. I'm scared. Please come home. There's something outside my window.

Agent Gallo swung back around and his face, stained with tears, was warped with a savage intensity of fear and rage. He raised the gun and took aim at Rook and fired.

In the flash of the shot, Rook had bounded across the beach towards them. Gallo fired again, and there in the second flash Rook was beside him and his hand clamped down hard on Gallo's neck and twisted.

As Gallo's legs gave out, Evan pulled his hands from his pants and then shrieked as Gallo fell over on top of him face first into the snow.

Rook pulled Gallo off and saw the blood, and then he saw Evan's hand and the shiv stuck deep in Gallo's belly. Evan was panting and shivering.

Rook rolled Gallo out of the way and lifted Evan into his arms and walked clear of the snow-swept beach into the safe gloom of the trees.

CHAPTER SIX

Rook carried Evan back to the SUV, feeling the child's heartbeat drumming hard. It had a clear double beat. When they reached the car, Rook tried the doors, but they were locked. He set Evan down on his feet.

"Stay here," he said.

Evan turned his face away from the wind, huddling against the car. Rook sprinted back through the trees and out onto the beach. The flashlight lay in the snow, illuminating a flat half-circle in which could be seen the two bodies. Rook reached them and knelt and felt the men's pockets and found the SUV keys underneath the white robe. He hurried back.

He lifted Evan into the back seat and closed the door. Then got in the driver's seat and put the keys in the ignition and turned on the heat. The SUV's headlights came on, shining out over the water. Snowflakes drifted through the beams.

Rook turned around and looked at Evan. His face was flushed and his teeth chattered, but he looked unharmed. His right hand was dark and wet with blood.

"Stay inside the car," Rook said.

He stepped out and shut the door. Evan saw him cross through the beams of the headlights.

Again, Rook sprinted through the trees and out onto the beach.

He came to the half-circle of light and the bodies and he picked up the flashlight and shone it over the snow. He found the bible and the gun, and wedged the big revolver in the back of his pants. He looked at the bible for a long moment and then replaced it gently on the ground.

Rook turned off the flashlight and put it in his coat pocket. Then he grabbed both men, each by an ankle, and dragged them across the beach and through the trees to the car. There, he stacked them against a tree.

He walked to the front of the SUV and out into the glow of the headlights towards the water. He took the gun from the back of his pants and threw it into the lake and threw the bible in also. When he turned around the lights were in his eyes. He walked again to the SUV and opened the back seat and gave the flashlight to the boy. Evan took it without a word. Rook shut the door again. He had not found the boy's shiv and he had cared little to look, assuming it was somewhere deep inside the Novitiate's stomach.

Evan sat and held the flashlight but he could have been holding anything or nothing. He could feel only the thick, cold, drying blood on his hand. A sudden gust of cold wind blew over the back of his neck and shoulders and he trembled and drew closer to the heaters. He looked again through the gap in the seats and saw Rook standing in the opening of the trunk.

In the trunk's cargo area, there was a large black duffle bag and a red can of gasoline. Rook rifled through the bag and found a length of rope, a white and red sash, two wooden crucifixes, and a black wool peacoat. He left everything and closed the trunk.

When he got back into the driver's seat, the car was warm. The windows had lightly fogged. He turned the heat down. He leaned across the passenger seat and opened the glove compartment. There was a map, a pack of gum, and a box of .357 Magnum bullets. He tossed the gum over the seat to the boy and closed the compartment. Then he pulled back the door handle and once more started to get out.

"Stop," Evan said.

Rook paused and looked over his shoulder.

"Can you just wait?" Evan said.

Rook pulled the door closed. He sat in the front seat and rested his head back. From behind him, he heard the boy sniffling and he heard him begin to cry. Rook closed his eyes.

Between sobs Evan said, "Who was she?"

"Who was who?"

"That little girl out there. Who was she? Is she all right? Did she get shot?"

In all the commotion and the need to get Evan safe, Rook had forgotten about the little girl. Or rather the *vision* of a little girl. What power had summoned her phantom he could hardly guess, but he knew it was far beyond his own conjuring.

"The little girl's all right," he said.

Evan sniffled and said, "Did I kill the man?"

"No."

He started to cry again. "But I stabbed him."

"You didn't kill anyone," Rook said. "I broke his neck before he fell. There's no need for tears. He was going to kill you."

Evan wept even more.

"Just calm down," Rook said. "You're all right."

"She was his daughter," Evan said, wiping his nose with his sleeve. "Wasn't she? The little girl."

Rook shrugged. "I don't know," he said. "Why do you say that?"

"She called him on the phone when we were driving. She was scared about going to sleep. She wanted him to come home."

"You heard her on the phone?"

"And then he was thinking about her out there. He was scared for her. When he saw you, he thought you hurt her. He was really scared for her."

"That's enough," Rook said.

"She was his daughter."

"I said that's enough."

They both fell silent.

Rook watched the snowflakes drift like silver through the beams of the headlights, and he could hear the low roar of the wind beyond the glass. As he watched the falling snow he thought about each flake as it fell and considered the many particular paths of descent. The slow side-to-side drift of their perpetual fall. Each one upon the same invisible current that all things follow—those priests, the boy, the little girl, one day even himself—each drifting along at last to land upon a hard surface and dissolve and vanish into nothing.

After a few minutes he rolled his head to the side and glanced back at Evan and saw he was asleep. Rook turned out the headlights and lowered the heat. He stared out at the dark of the lake and then in the windshield he saw his own face reflected, and so he shut his eyes.

CHAPTER SEVEN

Rook sat and watched the grey light of dawn come up over the eastern edge of the lake, and then he roused Evan and told him to get out of the car. Together they stood in the early dark and Evan shivered. Rook opened the trunk and took out the wool peacoat and the can of gasoline. He told Evan to take off his torn and bloodied jacket, and then he dressed him in the peacoat. It hung past Evan's knees. Rook folded up the sleeves and told Evan to button it. Then Rook walked to where he had stacked the two dead priests at the edge of the trees and he dragged both bodies to the back of the SUV and lifted them one at a time and stuffed them into the trunk. He opened the can of gasoline and doused the bodies and the interior and tossed the canister inside once emptied. He stepped back and motioned for Evan to step back also. The boy remained at the rear of the SUV, trying with numb fingers to turn up the collar of his new coat.

"Evan, come here," Rook said.

The boy obeyed, rubbing his eyes.

Rook cupped his hand over his mouth and sucked in a breath and blew it out again. He did this twice more and then and a puff of smoke escaped his closed fist. When he opened his hand there was a small flame in the centre of his palm. Evan watched and his mouth came open.

Rook steadied the flame in his hand, and then popped his wrist and the small flame drifted forward as if carried on a slight breeze. When it reached the open trunk, the flame spread like wildfire.

"Come on," Rook said.

They had walked a fair distance from the SUV when the vehicle exploded. Evan jumped, feeling the great rush of the heat against his back. He stopped and turned around and the sight of the flames seemed to awaken him as no force of light or heat ever had before. He stood in a kind of trance, hearing the crackle and roar and sizzle of the flames, and he felt naked and exposed and also cleansed. Where the heat of the fire touched him, something inside him seemed to reach out and touch it back. It was a tingling sensation, and it made him want to look deeper into the flames as if looking into a mirror. There was something special about the fire, and he was reminded then of a dream he often had—a nightmare—in which he was running from something, running as hard as he could, until finally he came to a great blaze of fire—and a man.

He looked up at Rook. A sudden impulse to take Rook's hand overcame him, but he stayed still. Rook glanced at Evan and saw that the child was smiling.

"Why are you smiling?" he asked.

"I'm smiling?" His voice drifted unawares.

"Are you hungry?"

Evan nodded. "Yep."

They turned from the burning vehicle. Ahead of them was a long narrow road and they walked side by side in the grey morning light, the boy waist height to the man. In the distance, the city was hushed and still dark. Evan dragged his feet.

"Quit that," Rook said. "Lift your knees."

They followed the long road out to Lakeshore Boulevard and after a short time they found a Tim Hortons bakery. The restaurant was empty save for two young women behind the service counter, brewing coffee and loading trays of muffins and donuts into the display cabinets. Rook ushered Evan straight into the washroom.

The overhead lighting was yellow and sterile. Rook washed Evan's hands and face with warm water and then he washed his own. The bathroom mirror had the circled streaks of a recent spray-and-wipe and Evan spit a mouthful of water up onto the glass. Rook raised an eyebrow. Evan stood with his dripping hands held out, a small grin on his face. Rook handed him a paper towel and they both dried their hands and faces together.

Evan said, "I got to *go.*"

Rook looked down at the boy. "Then go," he said.

Evan went into one of the stalls. Rook heard the latch click over. He stood and waited.

"Are you waiting?" Evan said.

"Yes."

"I can't go when you wait."

Rook looked confused.

"Are you still waiting?" Evan said.

"Yes."

"But I can't go. Can you go outside?"

"No."

"Please."

Rook huffed. "I'll give you one minute," he said, and he went out and stood just beyond the door with his back against the wall. He turned his head to listen.

He waited. He watched the employees behind the counter in their brown and beige uniforms and their slim visors that hid their eyes. The two young women moved in tired motions and seemed unimpressed. They were talking, but Rook heard nothing of what they said. One of them laughed and then tried to pinch the other's hip.

Rook looked past the two women to the windows. The sun was coming up on the glass, pale and pink and grey.

From inside the washroom, Rook heard a toilet flush. The taps at the sink ran. The sound of the water running lasted a while. Rook considered the windows and the advancing sunlight. Still the taps ran.

Finally, Rook reached for the door, but right then it swung back and Evan came out.

"What were you doing?" Rook said.

"I had to do a number two."

Rook nodded.

Evan giggled.

"Come on," Rook said, taking his hand. "Keep your eyes on the floor."

Rook bought a box of muffins and donuts and a bottle of water. The young woman who had laughed earlier served them at the cash. As she handed over the box of muffins, she said, "Does your son want a free Timbit?"

Rook looked down at Evan and hesitated. Evan stared at the floor.

"No, he's fine," Rook said.

They sat at a two-seater table away from the counter, and Rook told Evan to eat quickly. Evan had a few bites of a fruit-filled muffin and stopped. Rook kept his eye out the window and on the door. They were both silent. A pigeon bobbed along the curb outside, pecked at something, and bobbed along again.

Evan made a popping sound with his lips, holding his muffin in his lap. He said, "Why did you throw away that gun?"

"I hate guns," Rook said. "There isn't anything more terrible in this world than a gun."

Evan popped his lips again. "Why did you blow up the car?"

"Keep your voice down," Rook said with a glance to the young women behind the counter. Then, "They would have been able to track it."

"Who, those men?"

"Others like them. It's a whole organization."

Evan started to eat again. "Were they priests?" he asked.

"In a way, but not the kind that would ever hear your confession."

"What's confession?"

"They weren't regular priests," Rook said.

"They had crosses on their necks."

"That doesn't make a man holy."

"What about the people in the hotel?" Evan asked. "Who were they?"

At first, Rook said nothing. Then he sighed and turned to the boy. "I'll explain this once, so you listen. For the last six months, I've been looking for you, but so have other . . . people. What I didn't know was that they were following me, and it seems I led everyone straight to you. If we're lucky we won't have any more trouble. But you keep your eyes open and stay by my side. There might still be others out there hunting you."

The boy looked down at his lap.

"Finish your muffin," Rook said.

After a little while Evan started eating the muffin again. He ate another one and two donuts. He drank his water bottle. Rook folded up the box and left it. They gathered themselves and went out and started walking west.

They walked a long way along the side of the highway and then went under the overpass and crossed onto the Queens Quay. They continued west.

"Where are we going?" Evan asked.

"To catch a train."

— • •

When they finally reached Union Station the city had awoken and the streets and sidewalks were busy. Rook kept Evan close, holding his hand. He tried to keep to the shadows but they were shrinking fast. They entered the concourse and Rook scouted for police.

He saw them.

He stepped back behind a square column and pulled Evan with him. The concourse was busy. Over the endless sea of bobbing heads, Rook had seen a group of five police officers standing next to a bank machine, chatting. They had seemed casual, but they were vigilant, surveying the crowd.

What the hell am I doing? Rook thought. *This will never work.* Shaking his head, he forced away his doubt and focused on his reward. He tried to picture Allison's face. She would be there at the end of all of this. *Just get the boy to the church.*

Rook peered out at the officers again and then turned and took Evan's arm and went out.

They walked back down towards the lake and stopped when they reached the Queens Quay under the highway overpass. The nearest crosswalk was out of sight. Rook waited for a gap in the traffic and then he pushed Evan to start across.

Evan wiggled from under his hand. Rook reached and grabbed him, but Evan struggled.

"What the hell are you doing?" Rook said.

"You keep pushing and pulling me," Evan said. "I don't like it."

Rook stopped. A new stream of traffic was driving past. They stepped back from the curb. For a while they said nothing, only stared at each other.

Then Evan said, "You don't have to push me. I'm coming with you."

"You're not going anywhere else, that's for damn sure."

"You think I'm going to run away."

Rook scowled and glanced at the passing traffic.

Evan craned his neck straight up to look at Rook and said, "I saw those cops back there. I could've screamed, but I didn't. I didn't, okay? I'm coming with you. But I don't want to be pushed anymore."

"Are you about done?"

"There are mean people after me. People that are trying to get me. But you won't let them get me. Right?"

"That remains my choice."

"I got a choice, too," the boy said, sounding proud.

Rook looked down at the child and scratched his chin through his beard. Evan waited.

"Okay," Rook said. "I'll stop pushing you. But be smart and do as you're told. Got it?"

Evan nodded, a small grin escaping him.

Rook looked to the street. There was a gap in the traffic. Without much thought, he reached out to push Evan forward again, but he stopped himself. Evan glanced up at him with an expression that, under reversed circumstances, would have fit well on Rook's face. Rook nodded. They crossed the street to the median beside one another.

They sat down on a large weathered concrete partition under the highway overpass. It was cold in the shadow and the windswept snow covered it. The rush and noise of the traffic overhead was deafening in waves. Gazing up, Evan wondered if the highway would collapse. A stream of cars and trucks drove past on their right and then another in the opposite direction on their left. There seemed no end to the tumult of traffic and Evan, watching it all, felt dizzy and almost sick in the midst of all the motion.

He looked at his palms and he looked up at Rook. He inched closer to the man, as his large body seemed to block the wind and emit its own measure of warmth.

"Come on," Rook said, getting to his feet.

Evan got down and followed Rook to the curb. Rook was eyeing the traffic coming down the hill from the city. He knelt and spoke close to Evan's ear.

"When it stops, do exactly as the driver tells you."

"When what stops?"

"The bus. Do exactly as the driver says. Do you understand?"

"Okay," Evan said.

The traffic was coming down the hill swiftly now. Evan saw a Greyhound bus at the top of the hill, but it was still far away behind lines of traffic. His hands started to sweat in the cold, and he was feeling scared. How was he supposed to do what the driver told him? He didn't think the bus would ever stop for them.

All of a sudden Rook stumbled and put his hand on Evan's shoulder. His legs slackened and he held onto the boy for support. Evan struggled, bracing Rook with both hands.

"What's wrong?" Evan said.

The traffic on the hill slowed and brake lights shone red and car horns honked. Evan looked up and saw the Greyhound bus cutting into the left lane towards them.

It was going to hit them, Evan thought. He tried to step back from the curb out of its way, but it was difficult to move under Rook's weight.

"Mr. Rook," Evan said. "Look out!"

Rook groaned and slumped harder against him. Evan heaved his weight into Rook's chest to knock him back out of the way, but at that moment the bus pulled to a halt upon the curb of the median.

The driver slid the side window ajar and stuck his head out. He stared straight ahead as if looking at nothing. Then he said, "Get on the bus. Come on. Let's go, hurry up!"

Evan stood still, staring up at the driver and half-holding Rook. Then he felt Rook's hold on him tighten, and he remembered his instructions, Rook's words. His expression tightened with resolve.

"We're coming," he shouted up to the driver.

Evan started off the curb with Rook's hand on his shoulder, Rook stumbling and groaning. Cars honked and pulled around the bus and Evan heard indiscernible shouts and calls after them, swears and curse words he knew and remembered from the tongue of his foster father.

They came around the front of the bus and Rook grabbed the door and Evan slid out from under him and ran up the steps. The driver kept staring out through the windshield and said nothing, nor did he acknowledge Evan's entrance in any way. Rook lumbered into the bus after him.

They edged down the aisle and Rook used each headrest as a leaning post. The startled, uncertain passengers acknowledged the boy and the man with looks of curiosity, annoyance, and suspicion.

Evan went all the way to the back of the bus to find two open seats; the rest were taken. Rook waited until Evan had crawled across to the window and then flung himself down. He put his head back against the rest, closed his eyes, and let out a deep breath as if he'd been holding it this whole time. He groaned. The bus was put into gear rather suddenly and it lurched into motion.

Evan sat and watched Rook. He saw a line of blood run from

the man's nose. Rook's hand came up and wiped it away. Then, slowly, Rook opened his eyes. The bus was lugging up the ramp onto the freeway.

Evan whispered, "Are you okay?"

Rook wiped his nose again. He breathed easy. But he said nothing.

Evan watched him with worry. His hands were still sweating, and he wanted Rook to answer him.

After a moment, he said, "Mr. Rook, what happened to you?"

"Just be quiet," Rook said.

Evan narrowed his eyes and then he turned away and crossed his arms and looked out the window. The bus drove smoothly. Along the highway the traffic was even. The sun had risen well into a blue sky and there were only a few loose and thin clouds gathering. Evan watched the city transform into the passing of unknown streets and buildings, blurred into a grid of grey and silver motion at once enormous and miniscule. It seemed a faraway place.

Evan turned his head to look out the windows across the aisle and through the shifts of clouds he saw the lake, shimmering in the sun, and at times it looked as if the water was on fire. Streams of oncoming traffic flowed before this mirage and Evan pictured a conveyor belt of stars. There was an unusual familiarity to it all that he could not understand, and yet it comforted him.

"I've never left the city before," Evan said, more to himself than anyone else.

Rook looked down at him. "Your parents never—" The words dried in his mouth, as he realized what he was saying.

Evan said nothing at first. When he spoke next, Rook thought he sounded older than his years.

"They weren't my real parents," Evan said. "I got placed with them a year ago."

"You're an orphan?"

Evan nodded. He was quiet, gazing out the window. Then he said, "The man wasn't very nice to me. He never really wanted me around. He used to call me *money*. The lady didn't really want me either, but she pretended sometimes, at least. She was nice. Adam would always just put me in my room. Even if I didn't do anything. He'd get really mad at me and sometimes he would get really mad at Evie, too, but only when she would have a freak out and start throwing out all their stuff and saying she wanted to get better and cleaned up. Then Adam would get really angry and chase after her until she locked herself in the bathroom, and then he'd come after me and she wouldn't stop him."

He paused and trailed his finger along the window casing. Then he said, "One time Evie took me to this big plant place inside a glass house and it was all misty and warm when it was snowing outside. The plants were so big and there was one kind that had red leaves that looked like tongues and Evie told me it was a man-eating plant and if you got too close it would eat you. She took me for waffles after, too. Adam was working that day. That was a nice day, at least."

Rook asked, "You don't know who your real parents are?"

Evan shook his head. Then he said, "I know a bit. I know she was a farmer."

"A farmer? You mean your mother?"

"That's what they said. Adam said he read it in my file. It said I was found in a farmer's field with her."

"And she was your mother?"

"Yep. But she died."

Rook took a breath as if drawing back from the boy's comment and shook his head. "Nothing's ever free," he said, sounding tired. "Not a life, a breath, nothing. Someone always pays the cost."

Evan looked up at Rook and waited until the man returned his gaze. Then in a whisper, he said, "Mr. Rook, what—"

"Just call me Rook."

Evan paused. "Okay," he said. "Rook, what happened to you back there?"

"We got on the bus."

"But why did you fall over? And how did you know the bus was going to stop? Do you know the driver?"

"I do now," Rook said and winced as if from a headache.

Evan sat and watched him, his small brow furrowed, and he scanned Rook's face, eyes darting, as though the answer lay within the intricacies of the man's ragged skin. Rook saw Evan studying him.

"You really want to know?" he asked.

Evan gave a clear nod.

Rook leaned down to the boy and whispered. "I made a link between the driver and myself. It was weak because I did it during the day. That's why I needed you help. It took almost everything out of me. It would've been stronger if I'd conjured it at night."

Evan said nothing, but his eyes widened.

Rook said, "I went inside the driver's mind. I took control of him. I *was* him for a few moments. And I made him stop the bus."

"You were the driver?"

"That's right," Rook said again. "But there was a price."

"A price?" Evan whispered, as if it were a great secret.

Rook nodded. "It cost a piece of my own memory."

"How much?" Evan asked.

"It depends how long I'm away from myself." Rook shifted and pulled his coat tails out from under him. He went on. "The longer I stay in another's mind, the more memory I must give. If I stay too long, I risk forgetting who I am completely. Becoming lost. This has happened to others. They get trapped inside someone else's mind and go mad."

Evan nodded. He felt he understood, but could think of little to say. He was picturing a sick-looking child, thrashing in bed while all around stood priests and doctors.

Finally, he said, "Do you have to give up a nice memory?"

"I don't know," Rook said. "I can't remember."

The bus drove on and for some time neither of them, nor anyone it seemed, said a word. From one of the seats ahead music played, muffled through the headphones of a sleeping passenger. Outside the windows, the city had vanished and there were now expanses of snow-covered fields and a distant ridge of rock and trees.

After a while, Evan said, "Mr. Rook—I mean Rook—where are we going?"

"Shade's Mills," Rook said.

"What's that?"

"It's a small town not too far from here."

"Why are we going there?"

"We're going to meet someone."

"Who?"

"Someone at a church."

"Who are we meeting?"

Rook realized he didn't have an answer to that. He said nothing.

"Rook?"

"Yes."

"Do you have a family?"

"I did."

"What happened to them?"

Rook's expression darkened. "That's enough chatter," he said.

Evan started to ask another question, but right at that moment the bus swerved hard into the left lane. The driver gripped the steering wheel and pulled it back fast, his knuckles white. His heart raced as he steered the bus safely again into the centre lane. He let out his breath.

As soon as the bus was steadied, Rook sat forward and looked up and down the aisle. The light on the windows had changed. It seemed a cloud had formed over the highway, or the glass was repelling the sunlight. Rook was alarmingly aware that they were trapped inside a speeding bus.

The driver held their course, cruising, along Highway 401, southwest through The Ontario Greenbelt. The shadow Rook had noticed, or thought he'd noticed, lifted from the windows and the sunlight came back against the glass.

But something was different. Rook could feel it. The air inside the bus had changed. It was denser and heavier to breathe. Rook sniffed, catching a trace of smoke and sulfur like burning eggs.

Something had entered the bus.

Rook sat up straight in his seat. He touched Evan's arm, and the boy looked up at him and saw the gravity in Rook's eyes and became nervous himself.

"What is it?" Evan whispered.

"Stay calm," Rook said.

There was an elderly woman in a blue shawl sitting three seats up the aisle from them and, slowly, she began to turn.

Rook leaned out into the aisle and glanced down the length of the bus. At the same time, three other passengers also leaned out in unison and stared right back at him. Rook sat back abruptly.

Evan pulled at Rook's sleeve. "What is it, Rook?"

"We have to get off this bus."

He took Evan's hand and started to get up, but froze. The

elderly woman in the blue shawl had twisted around completely in her seat to face them. Rook swallowed hard.

The old woman's eyes were gone. In their place were two burned-out, blackened holes. It made her seem hollow and lifeless and yet she was still moving. Everyone was moving. Rook watched as more passengers turned, eyes the same burned-out holes, all of them twisting together in a horrid and unnatural unison.

"Come on, Evan," Rook said, pulling his hand.

Evan started. At the same moment, the passenger behind him rose from her seat. It was a young girl, perhaps twelve years old, with whitish-blonde hair in pigtails. When she reached her arm over the headrest, Evan turned and looked into her charred eye sockets. Her hand gripped his sleeve.

Evan screamed.

Rook had been watching the others, but he turned fast. He saw the little girl's grip on Evan's sleeve and right away smashed his fist across her arm and heard it break. Then he grabbed Evan and lifted him into his arms.

Braced against Rook's shoulder, Evan caught a glimpse down the length of the entire bus and witnessed a savage moment as every passenger, eyeless and horrible, came climbing and clawing over the seats, moving as one great roiling mass to get at them.

"Go, Rook!" Evan cried. "Go!" And he buried his face into the crook of Rook's neck.

He heard and felt Rook moving, hustling past the last few seats to the very back of the bus. Rook's strong arm tightened around his waist.

"Hold onto me," Rook said.

Evan wrapped his arms around Rook's neck and kept his eyes closed. He tried to think hard about what was happening, to make this all stop. He thought about the driver and the girl with the pigtails, tried to hear them in his special way, but what came to him was not a voice as he had ever heard before. It was a monstrous howling scream, and Evan physically recoiled from it, almost falling from Rook's arms. He couldn't bear to try again.

The bus swerved again and there was a violent tumbling of bodies, and Rook jammed his foot against the side of a seat to keep from going over. Evan's eyes opened instinctively. In that moment, he saw every passenger toppled together, surging and clawing like some wormy mass, and at the front of them he saw the driver. The man's eyes were charred like the rest, and his face was gouged and bleeding. Evan buried his face in Rook's neck, unable to witness anymore.

But the driver continued, pressing ahead of the rest, his arms outstretched and reaching like some grotesque supplicant caught between fealty and defiance.

The bus was lurching into the highway shoulder, the guardrail rising up before them rapidly.

As the driver clambered within reach, Rook grabbed the man's head and slammed it twice against a headrest and flung him back down the aisle. The others recoiled and then surged towards him and Evan again.

Rook hitched Evan firmly against his shoulder and reached up to the ceiling of the bus with his free arm. Evan looked up and watched Rook's hand grip the red lever on the emergency exit hatch, and then pull down.

There was a sharp pop above them and a rush of sucking wind, the force of which made Evan turn away. He felt himself raised up through the opening, and the sunlight was bright on his face. He could barely keep his eyes open against the wind, and he thought the force of it would blow him away, but Rook held him from below. Evan pressed his hands flat on the top of the bus, wishing he had something better to hold onto. Then he felt Rook climb up behind him. Rook's hands hooked under his armpits and he was lifted and gathered against Rook's chest. He could feel Rook's coarse beard on the back of his neck. The grip was almost suffocating.

"Hang on!" Rook shouted over the wind.

And then they were moving—flying—falling—and Evan saw the bus go upside down and far away. Rook's arms surrounded him, holding him so tight. They hit the hard gravel shoulder of the highway and rolled.

CHAPTER EIGHT

The bus crashed through the guardrail, tearing a four-foot gash across the outside baggage compartments. It turned over on its side in a cloud of snow and dust and slid to a halt in the ditch and the exposed tires spun in the air.

No more than a quarter kilometre back, Rook had landed in the snow-filled ditch at the highway shoulder with Evan in his arms. He got Evan to his feet and they hustled through the break of frozen wild grass and across the field into the woods. Once more they heard the sound of sirens behind them, but neither looked back.

Within the cover of the snow-tipped pines, Evan stopped running and stood. He put his weight on his left leg. A few feet ahead of him, Rook had stopped as well. His coat sleeve was torn at the shoulder, and his arm hurt from the fall. He rolled his shoulder in a slow circle to ease out the pain. At the same time, he surveyed the woods, sniffing the air. There was the cold dry smell of the winter below the pines and a deeper chill like death and nothingness that came with the wind when it blew, and also a tangy fecal musk of something feral. Rook rubbed his face with both hands and squinted out against the immense insecurity of the woods. He looked for where the snow seemed thinnest.

Behind him, Evan stood in the same place. He was shivering and he turned his face away from the cold at his cheeks. With both hands he gripped his right leg just above the knee, where his pants were torn and bloodied.

Rook looked back and saw him. "Come on, Evan," he said.

"It hurts really bad," Evan said, the start of tears in his voice.

Rook walked to Evan and knelt. "Move your hands," he said.

He pulled back the torn, bloodied denim and brushed some gravel from the wound. Evan winced. Rook picked up a handful of snow and cupped it over Evan's knee and held it there for a moment and when he took it away there was blood but it looked cleaner. Rook stood.

"You'll be all right," he said.

"But it really hurts."

"We'll go slowly. We'll find a dry place and once night falls, I can make it better."

Evan was trembling and his eyes watered. "Why can't you make it better now?"

"It's not easy in the daylight. But I promise I'll make it better as soon as I can."

Evan was trying to nod, his face and lips bunched tight in the cold. He seemed furious about something, and then he started to cry.

"You'll be all right," Rook said.

Evan said, "They were going to get us."

Rook knelt again and took Evan by the shoulders. "Nothing is going to get you. Not while I'm around. Okay?"

Evan sniffled and wiped his face.

From beyond the trees, sirens rang out and Rook looked back through the tall pines and saw the flashing lights and the red shape of a fire truck on the highway. He turned to Evan, who was calmer now.

"Are you okay?" Rook asked.

Evan nodded.

"Let's go."

They started and Rook walked slowly. Evan followed, stepping when he could into the big prints Rook made in the snow. The pine trees they walked under were tall and the boughs were covered in heavy clots of snowfall and, with a hard wind, they would crack and shower down upon the ground and cause craters.

As they walked Evan's knee stung in the cold, and he was reminded of being at school. He saw his grade one teacher, Ms. Bechtel, her big red face like a strawberry, telling them all to come sit on the carpet. Evan hadn't wanted to sit on the carpet. He'd wanted to stay in the corner where he felt safe, away from the other kids, on his own. *You have to come to the carpet*, Ms. Bechtel would say. Her sharp, dry grip on his wrist. Her hard yank of his arm. Evan's knee stung, and he came back in the present. Thinking about it, he was happy he would never see mean Ms. Bechtel or any of those people ever again.

By midday they had traversed only a small portion of the countryside, crossing glades and low hills and skirting a narrow, frozen lake. They took a break at the top of a hill where the snow cover was less.

In the distance, Rook could see the high grey ridge of the eastern Niagara bluffs and the cover of tall, bare pines and that's where he wished they could be. He knew there were caves among the escarpment where they could rest.

He looked at Evan. The boy was toughing it out, and Rook was impressed. Young as he was, Evan was strong. In Rook's head, he heard himself say, "Coddle a boy not and you'll have a man in a month." Then he saw Allison shaking her head, and he heard her voice. "Coddle a husband not and you'll have a boy in an hour," she'd said with a smile, rocking their son in her arms. Rook closed his eyes.

Evan squeezed his leg, his knee still bleeding, and he shivered. Soon it would be dark and much colder. Evan was hungry.

Rook looked out from the hill and could see the highway snaking in the distance and figured they could backtrack and try to hitch a ride southwest. There had to be someone who ignored the news, some simple, unawares fool, or otherwise someone who wouldn't give a damn if he picked up the devil himself. It was possible. Rook turned to Evan.

"What do you want to do?" he asked.

The boy only stared, too cold to show the surprise he felt at being asked.

Rook walked to him. "There's a chance we could catch a ride if we go back to the highway. What do you think?"

Evan shivered. His lips were blue.

They started back towards the highway, cutting northeast out of the pinewoods and across a field where the snow was deep to Rook's knees and he trailed his steps together to carve a trench for Evan to follow behind him. Still, Evan lagged. Rook went back for him.

"I thought I told you to pick up your feet," he said.

Evan shivered. His teeth clattered as he said, "What happens if they catch us?"

"Who?"

"Will the police will shoot you?"

"They might try."

Evan stopped.

"Let's go," Rook said. "We're wasting time."

"If we go back, they'll catch us. You'll get shot dead and I'll end up back"—he looked vaguely in the direction of the city—"back there. Then the mean people will find me!" His face was bright red and tight and trembling.

"Then what do you want to do?"

The boy began to cry again. "You're supposed to be in charge," he said.

Rook glared at him. He stood hunched and massive. His beard was frozen white with ice and spittle and his dark hair hung stiff before his face. He huffed once. Then he lifted Evan over his shoulder and took off at a run back towards the trees.

Thinking he had been about to get smacked, Evan hung over Rook's back with a feeling of surprise and relief, staring down at the clots of snow kicking up off Rook's big boots.

• • •

The sun was going down when they reached the top of the ridge. A frosty gloom enveloped the brush of the forest trail, paths once forged by hunters and nomads now relegated to dog-walkers and reckless youth. Below the canopy, the wind was less and the snow was sparse and speckled with pine needles and decayed leaves. The cold, dormant sense of the wintered earth was made all the more potent by the rich smell of the damp granite rock beneath. Rook walked slowly. Evan had fallen asleep over his shoulder.

Rook came to a break in the brush and there was a snow-swept gully that led down to a lower ledge on the cliffside. He secured Evan over his shoulder with his right arm wrapped around the boy's waist, and then scaled down the gully. The rocks were slick with ice, but after some careful shuffling he came out eastward on the lower ledge. The cliff looked down to the highway and the township of Halton Hills. Far out in the distance, Rook could see the piercing towers of Toronto's skyline and below that man-made ridge, the lake looked handsome with a wreath of clouds upon the horizon and the water catching a crimson sparkle in the falling sun.

Rook walked for a while along the outcropping before he found a slim recess in the rock. He lowered the boy into his arms like a bundle of wood and crouched and looked inside. The recess was low and it went back only about six feet before closing off in a jagged, frozen point. It looked dry.

Rook laid Evan on the ground and then unbuttoned and removed his heavy coat and flattened it on the floor, lifting Evan onto it and pulling it closed around him. He tied the sleeves so it was snug like a bag. Then he stood and walked out to the cave mouth and studied the night.

The crimson was gone. A deep violet threaded a sky that turned dark blue as he watched. He felt the sure hand of the night begin to reach for him, but he didn't need it. Not right now. He glanced over his shoulder at the boy. Fast asleep. Then he went out.

When he came back, his arms were full and he laid all he had gathered on the floor of the cave. He set the stones in a circle and laid one larger log lengthwise across them, then positioned the smaller sticks as a tipi in the centre and laid two more logs aslant the first. Crouched beside the stones, he looked out of the mouth of the cave at the darkening and waited.

The sky turned from dark blue to indigo and then to all black, or as close as was possible this near the glow of city lights. He cupped his hands over his mouth and felt his body start to hum. He breathed in and out. His palms warmed.

Eventually a thin line of smoke escaped between his fingers. He opened his hands and the walls of the cave were lit with the dancing shadows of his fingers. A small flame was camped in the centre of his palm.

•

Evan woke to the smell of wood smoke and stone, and the warmth of a crackling fire. The light of the flames flickered across the walls around him. He was bundled tight in Rook's jacket and it smelled musky and strange and familiar all at once. He yawned and rolled over. There was a pile of logs and branches piled beside the fire. He sat up. Rook was sitting at the mouth of the cave, looking out.

Evan wormed his way out of the coat and drew up his knees and hugged them. It took him a moment to notice that the pain was gone from his leg. He looked at his right knee. The cut was all gone. At first he thought he must have hurt his other knee, but then he saw the scar. Flat and white as if he'd been burned. It was healed. Evan looked up at Rook.

Almost as if the boy had willed it, Rook turned around. Then he stood and walked to the fire and knelt and placed another log in the flames. Evan slid the heavy coat out from under him and pushed it across to Rook, but Rook ignored it.

"Are you hungry?" Rook said.

"Kind of."

"We should get moving soon."

"My leg's all better," Evan said.

Rook nodded. "I mended it best I could. It will scar. How are your feet?"

"They feel wet."

"Take off your boots."

Evan peeled back the Velcro straps and pulled them off.

"And your socks," Rook said.

Evan removed his socks and wiggled his toes. They were stiff. He stuck his legs out straight to the fire. Soon the bottoms of his feet were hot. Rook laid the wet socks on the stones and after a moment the socks began to steam, giving off a sweet, distasteful smell that Evan secretly enjoyed. He reached his hands towards the fire and rubbed his palms together. Rook watched him.

"Once you're warmed, we'll get going. We'll get you something to eat." Rook started to get up.

"Wait," Evan said.

Rook paused.

Evan asked, "Can't we just stay for a little bit and warm up?"

Rook waited a moment. Then he sat down across the fire.

"Thanks for fixing my knee," Evan said.

Rook nodded.

"How did you do it?" Evan asked. "It's like it never got cut at all. Was it like what you did before? I mean . . . did you use *magic*?"

"Hush up," Rook said.

They sat in silence for a while. The fire burned between them, the damp logs hissing, and they listened to the wind whistle beyond the mouth of the cave, streaking with snow. Evan sat with his hands in his lap and he stole glances at Rook without turning his head. Rook stared far off into the flames.

They had been quiet for some time when Evan heard the song. It was faint, like an earthly rumbling in the stone of the cave. But it was rhythmic. He heard it behind him at first, and then all at once it was everywhere, above and below him.

He drew in his feet. "What is that?" he asked.

Rook pulled his gaze from the fire. "What do you hear?"

"It's sounds like a drum. There's drumming from somewhere." Evan's shoulders went up, eyes darting around the cave.

"Ignore it," Rook said.

"But what is it?" Evan asked. He could hear it clear as if it were rain. It remained faint and faraway, a deep travelling echo, but he was certain that he heard it. Then there was more.

"There's voices," he said. "There's voices singing, Rook. You hear them?"

"It's the song of these cliffs," Rook said. "Sung by the spirits that belong to them."

"Are they coming to hurt us?"

"No. We should be fine."

"What do they want?"

"To be heard, I suppose. Not many people listen for such things."

Evan sat with wide eyes and listened to the song of the cliffs. He turned his head, following the sweep of the drum and chorus across the stone. The song rolled away after a while. Then silence again. The wind whistled.

"It's gone," Evan said.

Rook said nothing.

"Did you hear it?"

"Yes."

"You did? Why didn't you say so? Why can we hear it when most people can't?"

Rook looked at Evan across the fire. "I don't know," he said. He was thinking of when he'd first seen Evan's eyes, how they had flashed almost like fire. The feeling that he knew the boy from somewhere, somehow. "Consider yourself lucky," he said.

Evan hugged his knees again, his expression grave. "I think we can hear it because we're different," he said.

"You think you're different?"

"Yep." Evan shimmied closer to the fire. He picked up a small stick and tossed it into the circle and watched the flames lick and curl around it like they were hungry. Then he said, "I'm different from everybody. I can just tell. I can *smell* it. It's like how you can smell when a dog or cat's been in a place. Their skin and their hair and stuff. Their sweat. Their poo and pee. It was like that with all the homes and all the people. I knew they weren't like me and they never could be."

"Perhaps you haven't met the right people," Rook said, surprising himself with the comment.

Evan was silent for a moment. Then he said, "Sometimes when Adam would come after me, I'd lie there really still and think, *You can hurt me, you can hurt me all you want, but you can't kill me. You can beat me with your stinky hands, but that's all you can do because I'm bigger than you, I'm higher, and you can't ever get me at all.*"

"Did you hate them?" Rook asked.

Evan shrugged. "I felt bad for them. They were both really sad a lot. That's why sometimes I tried to use my special-thinking to make them feel better."

Rook straightened. "Your special-thinking?" he asked.

Evan nodded. "It's something I can do sometimes. I don't know how, but sometimes it happens. That's why I really know I'm different."

"What is it?"

Evan looked at the ceiling of the cave, titled his head. "It's like I think really hard about someone, sometimes I can make them do what I want."

"You've done this before?"

Evan nodded in big deep swoops and he seemed excited, proud, and embarrassed all in equal measure.

"Have you done it to me?"

Evan stilled. Then he shook his head. "I tried, back when you first . . ." He stopped and then said, "I don't like doing it, really."

"Why not?"

"Because of what I hear. When I think really hard about someone, then I hear their voice in my head. I hear them crying. Sometimes they scream."

For a moment Rook's expression was forlorn and revealing, as if he were catching splinters of a memory recently forgotten, a memory he would never, ever, fully recall. "I think I know what you mean," he said.

"You can do it, too, can't you?" Evan asked. "That's what you did to the bus driver. You made him do what you wanted."

"It's different," Rook said. "I didn't convince him to do what I wanted. I became him, then I acted through him."

"It's magic," Evan said. "We can both do it, and that's how I know *we're* different."

"I'm sorry, Evan, but I think you're wrong. This magic, if you want to call it magic, sends out signals when it occurs. It reverberates. It causes a ripple like when you throw a stone into water and others can feel it. I've felt no such ripple from you."

Evan frowned. "You don't think I can do it?"

"I didn't say that. But like everything else, magic is a way of getting through this world, only it's more like cheating your way through. You're cutting little holes in the fabric of it all to get through faster, easier. But those holes—each tear—makes a sound, sometimes it's big and sometimes it's small. When I cheat fire into my hand, that's nothing, barely makes a sound. But when I possessed the bus driver, I might as well have been ringing a bell."

Evan's face lost its colour all of a sudden.

"Are you all right?" Rook asked.

Evan tried to speak but trembled, wiped his nose, and spoke again. "Rook . . . what happened to all those people on that bus?"

Rook shut his eyes. "They were possessed," he said. "But hell if I know by what. It must have been something very old and powerful to take control of so many souls at once. I've never seen anything like it."

Evan asked, "Was it after me?"

"Yes."

"Where did it come from?"

"Somewhere none of us want to be."

"Is it going to come back and get us?"

"No," Rook said. "That was my fault. I should have known I was drawing attention. But I won't do that again. We'll be fine."

"What about my special-thinking?"

"I don't think you have that magic, Evan."

The child looked hurt, so Rook added, "Or if you do, some greater magic must be keeping you hidden. Either way, best to forget about it. Now hush up. Get ready to go. Put your socks and boots back on."

Evan picked up his socks one at a time and slipped them on his feet and then put on his boots. When they were strapped he stretched them out to the fire again. Rook was silent all the while, looking over his shoulder to the cave mouth.

Evan picked up a dry wood chip and tossed it at the fire. His eye hunted the floor for another and he tossed it in as well. Then he looked at Rook.

He asked, "Hey, rocks or fires?"

Rook turned. "What?"

"It's a game. You have to pick one. Rocks or fires?"

"I don't care."

"Just pick one, the one you like more. Right away. Go. Rocks or fires?"

"Rocks."

"Apples or bananas?"

"I've never had a banana," Rook said.

"Then you have to say apples. Okay, try again. Lunch or dinner?"

"Neither."

Evan frowned. "Play right," he said, then, "Dancing or singing?"

"Dancing."

Evan laughed. "Really? Okay, hunting or hiding?"

"Hunting."

"Night or day?"

"Night."

"Good guys or bad guys?"

"Good."

"Monsters or angels?"

"Monsters—"

Evan stopped. He looked at Rook straight across the fire. His mouth opened as if preparing to speak, but then it closed. He pulled in his feet and sat crossed legged and looked in the fire.

Then he looked at Rook again. He asked, "Rook, do you believe in God?"

Rook was taken aback. Lost for words. Not for the first time, he felt that Evan spoke with thoughts far beyond his years.

Evan repeated, "I *said*, do you believe in God?"

"How old are you?" Rook asked.

"Six. Almost seven."

"You're too young to be thinking about God."

"I can't help it sometimes," Evan said. "Sometimes it's all I think about. I wonder where He is, what He thinks of me. Sometimes I pray, too. I ask Him for help, but I never hear anything." Evan quieted and flicked a piece of bark in the fire. Then he said, "I believe in God. But I don't understand why God lets people do bad things. Why doesn't God make everyone good? Why does God let the Devil hurt people?"

"You think it's the Devil that hurts people?"

"Isn't the Devil the bad guy?"

Rook looked caught by some impossible reckoning. He was reminded of a prayer, a plea, spoken long ago—and the voice that answered.

He said, "I heard someone say once that God gave the Devil the burden of evil. In the new world God had created, this world, people would have the will do as they thought was right, and in order for them to know goodness they had also to know evil. They had to hate and fear it. They had to know its name. So God looked to his angels and asked one of them to fall, to be cast out and hunted, to become the symbol of all evil for all time. It was the Devil that came forward and accepted the burden. Not because he wanted to hurt the world, but because he loved God."

"But why doesn't God just let the Devil be good again?"

Rook shifted and looked at the boy in the face. "Have you ever seen someone build a house?"

Evan thought about it. "There was a big building built across our street once."

"Did you see the construction workers? Men using hammers and tools? A man with a plan of blueprints?"

"There were dump trucks, and a big crane."

"Right. Well, when that building was finished, did the dump trucks stay across the street, or did they move on to the next job?"

Evan shrugged. "I guess they left."

"I think God did, too. I think he took off the day the work was done and left this house to the mercy of its myriad tenants."

Evan shook his head. "The mercy of its *what*?"

"Nothing. Like I said, you're too young to be thinking about these kinds of things."

Evan sat with a deep pensive look on his face. "Who told you all that stuff?" he asked.

Rook stiffened and although he sat in the glow of the fire he appeared withdrawn in shadow. "That's enough talking," he said. "It's time to leave."

Evan was surprised and he sat back. "Okay," he said, a little hurt and wondering if he'd done something wrong.

The fire had burned down to embers. Rook stomped the coals with his boots and kicked the ashes to the back of the cave and tossed the stones and the remaining logs outside. He waited until Evan was ready and then he turned and started out into the cold dark. Evan followed at his heels.

They had started back only a little way along the lower ledge of the escarpment when Rook saw the lights. At once he lowered and grabbed Evan's arm and pulled him to a squat. Below the ridge, the lights of the highway snaked and the town was a sprawling sparkled cloud. The red and blue flashing was sinister and serene.

Keeping low, Rook led Evan along to the gully and told him to hop on his back, and then Rook climbed back up the gorge and emerged on the trailhead. He set Evan on the ground and they cut from the path into the pines.

As if stepping behind a wall, the wind fell and the woods were silent. They could see their breath and the snow was dark blue.

"Wait here," Rook said.

Evan nodded. Rook walked back out to the trail and stood behind a tree at the top of the cliff and looked down. He could not see all the way but he gathered a fair impression of at least five police cruisers parked along the shoulder of the highway far below. He looked along the length of the trail to the hill where they had come up earlier. In every direction the woods were a deep bluish dark, and the trees had been shaken free of snow in the winds, standing black and skeletal, and for this at least Rook was pleased. It would make escape easier if they were spotted. Although he suspected the police would have dogs. He hurried back to Evan.

"Let's go," he said.

They started walking and the snow was deep but light and powdery. Rook sniffed at the air for any kind of scent beyond the cold dormancy of the earth. For the feral, bodily odours of man or animal. There were only faint traces. He paused, then, realizing how much his own keen sense mirrored Evan's claim to difference. *I can smell it,* Evan had said.

Perhaps the child had true gifts after all.

Whenever Rook caught even the slightest whiff of anything other than the clear open smell of dead winter, he led Evan in the opposite direction. Together they walked with haste and silence.

They came upon a clearing and below the dusting of snow odd bulbous shapes were arranged in varied rows. Evan stooped and lifted one and shook the snow from it. A thin covering of ice remained. It was all but black. They were small and stunted, half rotten.

"Leave it," Rook said.

"It's a pumpkin," Evan said.

"I said leave it."

Evan dropped the pumpkin into the snow and they started again. After a moment, Rook paused and put up his hand and turned to sniff the air. From the northwest came a strong smell of fur. But unlike the feral trace Rook had been expecting, this was a sterile aroma like soap. The scent of an animal that was groomed well and kept to live in a cage.

Evan watched Rook's hand, still held up in the air. The trees creaked in the silence. Evan was about to ask if everything was all right, when the first bark cut through the woods like a gunshot.

Then another bark answered, sounding like an echo. Rook and Evan turned around. The dogs were back somewhere along the trail, but they were coming up fast.

Yellow beams of light shone up through the dark canopy, swaying side to side. The dogs bayed now with the rushing excitement of the chase, and Rook knew they had been found. Unwashed, blood-covered, sweating—it had always only been a matter of time before the dogs had caught their scent. Rook heard the echoing voices of men below the swaying lights.

He looked to Evan. "Can you run?" he asked.

Evan nodded.

"Then do it."

They both started, running fast and kicking up a trail of powdered snow. The baying of the dogs spread out behind them. Evan kept running. The air was icy in his throat and each breath was a sting. He tried just breathing through his nose.

He stopped after a while and Rook came back to him.

"We need to hurry up," Rook said.

Evan nodded and wiped his nose. Behind them, the yellow lights shone out wide and the officers' voices called out to the dogs.

Rook considered their tracks back through the trees and shook his head. The police didn't even need dogs at this rate. He grabbed Evan under the arms and slung him over his shoulder.

Once more they took off through the snow. Ahead of them, a hill went down to a shallow glade through which a stream flowed east to the cliff side. A second hill rose up out of the glade and was capped with a deeper wood. They came upon the first hill and the snow on the slope was fine and powdery. Rook slid down on the flats of his feet.

At the bottom, Rook crunched through the sheet ice of the frozen stream and paused on the other side and looked back up the hill. The baying of the dogs was quieter. The sound dipped into the glade but it seemed far away. He could no longer hear the calls of the officers, and the canopy was dark above the hill. It was as if the dogs had caught different prey and gone off.

Rook set Evan down and they turned and faced the second hill before them. It was larger and steeper than the slope they had come down.

"Well?" Rook said, looking down at Evan.

"I can do it," Evan said.

"We'll keep on through the trees at the top."

Evan started upon the mount. After two steps he slipped on the ice and staggered, planting his hands into the snow. Then he stood and started again. The snow was deep and heavy in the glade. Rook waited a moment longer, surveying the hill, then followed behind him. He stepped wide to clear the ice of the stream into the snow. Then he stepped again and roared with pain as something tore into his ankle, twisting on his right leg and falling to a knee. Evan spun and slipped.

"What happened?" he cried out.

Rook sat on the ground, leaning forward with his hands wrapped around his right calf. His foot was trapped in a set of sharp teeth below the snow. Evan started down the hill towards him.

Rook saw him and said, "Get! Turn around and get up that hill. Keep going to the trees. I'll catch up. If I don't come, just keep running. You know what happens if they catch you."

"But—"

"Don't argue," Rook said.

Evan turned, reluctantly, and continued up the hill. His pace was slow but even and he reached the top. He looked down once and saw Rook watching him, and then he hurried on to the trees as told.

Rook waited until Evan was out of view and then he set his attention to his snared foot. He tried to pull in his leg but a sharp, striking pain stopped him.

Right then, he heard the renewed baying of the dogs. They were back on his scent. He looked up and saw the yellow beams of light casting through the tops of the trees.

He brushed the snow away from his ankle and revealed the full capacity of the trap. It was a rusty leg-hold trap with a six-inch steel mouth, fit for catching coyotes or wolves. The sight caused Rook's teeth to grind in anger at the thought of the person who had set it out here.

He gripped the two metal springs of the trap and squeezed them to release the jaws. His breath held—he squeezed with all his strength. The springs compressed and the teeth of the trap loosened from his bone, but the metal was sleek and wet from the snow and his hands slipped and the trap closed. The razor teeth bore into his ankle and he groaned and leaned back, the pain running up his leg to his hip. He tried again. This time he shook his foot as the springs loosened the teeth, but again his hands slipped and the trap bit into his bone. He let out a roar of unbearable pain that for a brief moment hushed the dogs.

• — •

Evan heard the roar but he stayed true to what Rook had told him and he kept running. A strong wind blew from the east edge of the escarpment and Evan tottered on tired legs and almost fell, but he gathered himself and pushed through it, his arm in front of his face. He entered a dense copse of spruce trees grown broad and full together and Evan had to crawl on all fours to escape the cold scratches of the needles on his face and neck.

Within the cover of the trees the wind was settled and it was almost warm. Evan sat and breathed through his mouth. He could hear very little from beyond them. Then, distantly, he heard the dogs. It sounded like a memory of a noise stuck in his head. He waited. His heart raced. He sniffled and wiped his nose on his sleeve. He wanted Rook to come.

Come on, he thought, hearing Rook's own voice in his head. *Come on.*

He listened to the dogs baying and they were louder and more excited and then he heard the voices of men calling. A faint yellow light was cast up into the trees around him and the spruce needles became stark and sharp looking. Evan shimmied back from the reach of the light. After a moment it dipped away to darkness. Evan's heart was pounding. He held his breath. Then for a moment all went quiet. He listened and hoped.

A gunshot fired.

Evan straightened. He was still in the silence that followed.

Then another shot fired, sweeping up through the trees and back.

All at once, Evan leapt up and started running away through the trees. The dense spruce opened into a broader forest of poplars and tall, thin pines that seemed to stretch out ahead of him forever. His calves burned, his right side cramped and his eyes became bleary with tears. But he ran.

Kicking up snow, churning his path into an unmistakeable sign of his flight, he felt in his heart that this was his life now. It felt like a dream, familiar and unbelievable, but it was no dream. Not anymore.

Here he was. He could see himself. Running.

It's real, he thought. *It's happening.*

He ran blindly, and the trees and the lights and the baying of the dogs were nothing but past ideas of things he'd once known. He ran without breathing, unable to stop, unable to hide, for nothing, not ever, would conceal him again nor offer him refuge from this world that had risen like the monsters from his secret nightmare to hunt him for all time.

He crossed a clearing and entered another thicket and ducked below the first branches. He darted between the trees in a sweeping serpentine motion and coming around a broad-reaching spruce, he turned and collided straight with a man's rear end and fell backwards on his butt in the snow.

Right away, he looked up and hoped and prayed for it to be Rook. But it was not. The man turned around, and he was tall and broad-shouldered. He wore a dark toque and a beige, waist-length coat with a thick fur collar. Evan could see little of his face. His hands were in his jacket pockets but at that moment he pulled them out and scratched the back of his neck.

"Shit," he said. "You all right, kid?"

Evan said nothing. The man's face was little more than a round shadow leering over him.

At that moment a second man stepped out from between the trees and joined the first. His shadowed form was slighter and shorter and the side flaps of his toque bounced as he walked like some long-eared dog.

"What's that, Al?" the second man asked.

"It's some kid."

"A kid? A boy or a girl?"

"Don't know. Just ran smack-dab into my ass." The man called Al turned to Evan. "You okay, kid? What you doing out here? You lost?"

Still Evan said nothing.

"You lost, kid?"

"Hey, Al," said the second man.

"What were you running for? Someone chasing you?"

"Hey, Al—"

"What?"

The second man stepped up close to the first. He cupped his hands together over his mouth and leaned against the first man's ear and said, "Christmas come early, eh?"

"Get off me," Al said and pushed the little man back. Then he turned again to Evan and stepped once forward and squatted. "Hey kid, listen, what are you doing out here?"

There was faint moonlight coming through the canopy and Evan could see the man's face a little better. He had a wide brow and it was creased in the middle like he had been thinking hard about something for a long time. The centre of his face was bowl-shaped and shadowed, as if his eyes and nose and top lip were all sunken back into his head. Evan had never seen any face like it and in a past life it might have frightened him. Through the gloom he saw the light blue colour of the man's eyes and they had a clear and thoughtful quality.

Evan said, "They were chasing me."

"Who was chasing you?"

"The police."

"The police were chasing you? You running from the cops, kid?"

Evan said nothing.

"Well, listen. I'm Al. I got a place not far from here. Why don't you come on with us? Get out of the cold. Get something to eat. I got a car, too. I can take you wherever you want to go. How's that sound?"

Evan looked down at his hands, bright red in the cold. His face was streaked with tears and his cheeks were stinging. His butt was wet from the snow.

The man waited. He looked once over his shoulder to his companion and then he turned back and regarded Evan singularly. His broad torso remained very still and his legs were sturdy and it seemed he could have squatted there for hours. His breath was soundless, like he lived without breathing at all.

After a while, Evan nodded. "Okay," he said.

"Okay," Al said and clapped his hands together. "Let's get you out of this darn cold. We got a big stew on. Then we'll drive you anywhere you got to go."

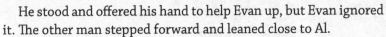

He stood and offered his hand to help Evan up, but Evan ignored it. The other man stepped forward and leaned close to Al.

"What about the traps?" he whispered.

"We'll come look tomorrow. Let's get the kid in."

The smaller man nodded and grinned and his gums showed above his teeth in the moonlight. They both turned towards Evan and looked down at him as he stood and patted the snow from his butt and rubbed his hands together. They watched Evan with eager smiles hidden behind the shifting shadows of their faces.

CHAPTER TEN

The two men led Evan a few kilometres northwest along the escarpment. The pinewoods cleared to open fields, flat and snow-swept and dark under the clouded night sky. From the distance, the noise of the highway hummed but their path itself was silent. They did not talk. Al led the way and Evan followed and the other, Kinny, walked in the rear.

When at last the cabin was in sight, Al let out a breath and said, "Home sweet home."

At first, Evan failed to see it. The cabin was small and covered in snow with makeshift shutters over the windows, and a small trace of the inner light shone out. A crude chimney pipe stuck up from the roof and Evan could see a trail of smoke escaping.

They approached from the east and came around to the cabin's sole entrance. A plain wood-framed door on brass hinges. The men stopped and shook off their toques. There was a blue tarp attached at the right of the door, tied taut between four posts, with a pile of felled pine logs underneath that were dusted with snow and damp. Looking past the entrance, Evan saw a big white van with black windows parked under a tree. Another smaller car sat just beyond the van, but it was buried in a snowdrift to the point of near invisibility within that wintered landscape.

Al unlocked the cabin door and swung it open and waited to its side like an usher. Evan hesitated on the threshold. He turned and looked back across the clearing, expecting and hoping to see Rook appear from the far woods and call him away. But the darkness held nothing save the drift of the snow in the wind and the erasure of their tracks. He turned back to the open door and the inner light, warm and welcoming as the smell of the cooking stove, and he stepped inside. Al and Kinny stepped in after him, and Al closed the door.

It was a shabby, two-room cabin built for the necessities of small-game hunting and little else. Right away, Evan could smell the stew in the air, taste it on his tongue. His mouth watered. There was a pot on the top of the wood stove, a full fire blazing within, and Evan watched the steam rising from the pot in streams of flavour swirling up through the air. The kitchen table was set with bowls as if to catch the steam as it thickened and tendered and dripped like gravy. Evan's hunger led him farther in.

The table was handmade out of wood planks, as were the counters and shelves that lined the walls, mismatched repurposed lumber full of many nails. Everything was covered in a fine layer of dirt or dust or grease, the sight of which somehow increased Evan's appetite. It was like being inside some butcher's rustic cookhouse. The dense air, trapped within the shuttered windows, drifted from the kitchen into the second room to coat the sheets and blankets of the bunk beds therein.

"Are your feet wet?" Al said.

Evan started as out of a daze and looked up at the large man. Then he looked at his feet. He nodded.

"Well, get those boots off and we'll hang your socks over the stove."

Al crossed the room and took off his tan jacket and hung it on the wall from a hook of antlers. He picked up what looked like a big green and brown blanket and swung it over himself and his head came through a hole in the middle and he wore it loose over his shoulders and it covered his body to his knees.

Evan took off his boots. Beside him, the smaller man, Kinny, was bent over at the waist, unlacing his own boots. Evan could hear the man sniffling. When Kinny had his boots off, he stood and wiped his hand across his nose and then across his pant leg. He grinned at Evan through his red patchy beard and his gums stuck out dark and pink. His right eye seemed like it was looking off to the corner of the room.

Al came over. "Give me those wet socks," he said.

Evan peeled off his socks. The floor was freezing on his bare feet, but he handed his socks over to Al anyway. Al held them at an arm's length and pinched his nose dramatically, smiling like a clown. A smile broke on Evan's face.

"There," Al said. "That's what I wanted to see. Come on and sit down."

Evan went around the side of the table and sat on a wooden bench that was little more than a tree trunk hewn in half. He pulled his feet up and gripped his icy toes. At that moment, a young girl came out of the second room. Evan looked up at her.

She was much younger than the two men, fourteen or fifteen, and yet Evan thought she somehow seemed very old. Her red hair was pinned up at the back and she was wearing a grey-green dress with a white shirt underneath rolled up to the elbows and a pair of dirty jeans and an apron. She went straight to the wood stove and picked up a wooden spoon and stirred the pot. Evan wanted her to turn around so he could see her face again. He was sure there was something unusual about her face and he wanted to know what it was.

Kinny went away into the second room. Al sat across the table from Evan and watched him. Hardly moving at all, he leaned down to the shelf at his side and lifted out a large clear jug with a rubber stopper and set it on the table.

"A glass, Mother Maeve," Al said.

The girl at the stove took a tin cup down from the shelf and crossed the room and set it on the table before Al. As she came, Evan looked up and saw her face clearly. He stared for a moment, and then he looked away.

Maeve's eyes were small and dark and her nose was upturned like the snout of a pig. Evan felt funny looking at her for long. She must have been in some kind of an accident. A scar ran from her top lip to below her right eye, slicing through her nose so the cartilage had healed strangely and curved upward. She glanced at Evan once, catching his eye. Then without a word she returned to the stove.

Al popped the stopper from the bottle and tilted it on its side and filled his cup. When the sharp odour came across the table, Evan put his head down as to avoid it. It reminded him right away of his foster parents. First that smell, then they got loud, and then they got mean. All at once, Evan wished he had never come with these people. He wished he had stayed outside in the cold and dark where he could run away. He looked to his socks hanging over the stove. They seemed very far away.

Kinny came back from the other room. When he saw the bottle on the table he stopped and made a knowing face and went out again. Then he came back carrying a clay cup and he sat down at the table beside Al. Evan saw letters etched on the side of the clay cup: *KINNY'S*. Kinny reached for the bottle but caught himself and looked at Al.

"Can I have some?" he asked.

Al said, "Well, I don't know, Kinny. *Can* you?"

Kinny's small brow furrowed. He said nothing.

"You got to say 'may I,'" Maeve said.

Kinny nodded and then giggled. "Oh, yeah. May I have some?"

"Of course."

Kinny slid his cup close to the bottle and tipped it over and poured. It trickled down the side of the bottle and pooled on the table. Al watched the pool, watched it start to sink into the wood. When Kinny finished, Al slid the bottle away and then dabbed his forefinger in the spill. He stuck his finger in his mouth.

Kinny sipped from his cup and looked sideways at Evan. Maeve stopped stirring for a moment and straightened her back and turned her ear as if expecting some higher presence to speak. Kinny saw her. He jumped up and crossed to the stove and looked over Maeve's shoulder.

"Did you keep the fat like I asked you, Mother Maeve?" he asked.

"I got it warming," Maeve said, tapping the rim of a small cast iron frying pan with the wooden spoon.

Kinny sniffed at the steam from the stove and licked his lips. "Oh good, Mother Maeve. Oh goodie."

Kinny turned around with a grin on his face, then returned to the table and sat. Next to him, Al was staring straight at Evan, his blue eyes unblinking. He dabbed his finger once more in the spilled liquor. It had all but seeped into the wood. He raised his finger and put it into his mouth. Then all at once he retracted his finger and shifted in his seat.

"So kid," he said. "Why were you running from the cops?"

Evan said nothing.

"Yeah, that's okay," Al said. "You don't have to tell us. Anyway, I hope you like rabbit."

"I was kidnapped," Evan said.

The small room fell quiet. Kinny glanced at Al over the rim of his cup.

"You were kidnapped?" Al said. "By whom?"

"His name was Rook," Evan said. He seemed all of a sudden to be on the verge of tears. "He came and took me away from the apartment in the city. He said I had to do what he told me. He said if I didn't do what he said he would kill me, but he was lying, because . . ." Evan wiped his nose with his sleeve. "Because when the mean people came after me Rook stopped them. He didn't let any of them hurt me. He protected me. But then . . . but then I thought we were safe but the cops found us, and Rook told me to keep running and I heard the gunshot. They shot him." Evan hung his head and wept.

Maeve had turned from the stove to study Evan. In a revelatory tone, she said, "You're the one on the news."

Evan sniffled and looked up. Maeve was staring at him like he was the only thing in the room. She held the wooden spoon in her hand. Her small dark eyes were wide and her mouth was open, sincere and shocked and somewhat marvelling.

"I heard about you," she said. "Everyone's out all over looking for you. The Toronto police, the Hamilton—" She stopped.

Al had turned in his seat and was regarding her thoughtfully. When she saw him, she closed her mouth and looked at the floor. Her whole body stiffened as if something had cooled her blood.

Al crossed his arms over his chest. He asked, "You *heard* about this kid? Where did you happen to hear about him, Mother Maeve?"

Maeve's mouth was tight and she breathed through her nose, her expression grave and hiding. Finally she said, "I just popped out to the van for a minute. I was looking to see if we had anymore chicken wire and I started it up just for the heat. That's all. The radio just came on. I swear."

"And you listened to it?"

"I just heard it while I was looking in the back."

"Go to bed, Mother Maeve," Al said.

"I swear. I didn't—"

"Go to bed. Now."

Maeve turned and dropped the wooden spoon into the pot and rushed into the second room and pulled the hanging curtain closed.

Al finished his drink. Then he took one of the bowls from the table and went to the stove and stirred the pot once and ladled stew into the bowl. He grabbed a metal spoon from the drawer and returned and set the bowl in front of Evan on the table.

"It's hot," he said. "Might want to wait a minute."

Evan had stopped crying. He sat very still, dried tears on his cheeks. He could smell the stew in the bowl in front of him and as before his mouth watered. He looked down. It was a greyish brown colour, like sludge, mostly potatoes and thin slices of meat. Rabbit meat. He lifted the spoon and blew on it and then ate hungrily.

Across the table, Al poured another drink. Kinny sat in silence, still sipping from his cup. They both watched Evan eat.

"Have you ever hunted?" Al asked.

His mouth full, Evan shook his head.

"I hunt regularly," Al said. "Well, I suppose you'd say I trap. I don't stalk the animals or chase after them. I set traps. And I don't use a gun, either. When I get an animal in one of my traps I kill it with a knife. I don't shy away from it. That moment. I don't shy away at all. I look the creature right in the eye and I say, 'I have caught you. I am a hunter and it is in my blood to hunt you and catch you, and now I have. Finally we have met each other as by our bloodlines we were destined to.' And I don't break the eye contact, not even when I slide my knife across the throat. That's real important. To watch that part. To see the life go out and to let that life see you taking it. It's something human beings have forgotten. That relationship between life and death. When you watch it, well, it's like life and death are screwing. But you don't know much about that."

He winked and emptied his cup in one gulp and refilled it.

Then he went on. "It's something crucial to us as a species. That relationship. I mean we are *killers*. The 'human being' is a hunter and hunters kill. That's what we are *naturally*. What we are supposed to be. It's in our bloodlines. And you know why? You know why we're hunters?"

Again, Evan shook his head.

"Because it's a game of intelligence. It requires a mind. Humans naturally excel at hunting. At least we did a long time ago. Now . . . I just don't know." He studied his tin cup for a moment. Then he said, "I use traps because a trap is like a human—"

"A trap is intelligent," Kinny said, echoing words he had clearly heard before.

"I'm speaking," Al said.

Kinny looked at the tabletop.

Al waited. Then he said, "A trap is intelligent. It's like a mind, waiting to spring. It's an extension of the hunter. Sure, some say trapping isn't hunting, that real hunting needs a rifle and a hunting dog, but that's just sport. Aiming and shooting a gun isn't intelligent, it's mechanical. It's lacking in nature. But a trap . . . now a trap is natural. For thousands of years our ancestors chased animals with rocks and sticks, but only when they learned to set traps did the human beings start to take over the world. A trap is the essence of intelligence. Human beings need to remember that." He filled his cup once more and gulped it and then swept his hand out as if over a vast expanse. He said, "Right now everywhere humans are stupid. They need to remember their intelligence, their *struggle*. Life is a struggle and humans need it to thrive. Right? The hunter struggles always, and his increase in intelligence is his reward. But right now we just coast around from life to life just thinking we are smart. In reality we have become weak and useless. And there are just so many of us now and nothing to do with a single one of us. And that right there is the dilemma."

Evan had finished the bowl of stew.

"Was that good?" Al said.

Evan nodded. He blinked and the feeling of his eyes closing was comfortable.

Al poured another drink and said, "I'm sorry you were kidnapped, kid. You got any idea why the guy picked you? I mean of all the kids out there, why you?"

Evan looked at Al in the face. And then, boldly, he said. "Because I'm different."

"Oh, you're different, eh? How's that?"

Evan pursed his lips, making a face as if he had an idea, but a yawn overcame him and he shrugged.

Al said, "I didn't think you would know. But I'll tell you the answer. The truth is there isn't any reason. You got kidnapped just 'cause. You're not special or different at all."

Evan shook his head. "But Rook was protecting me."

"Protecting you, eh? Well, now he's gone. So who's going to protect you now?"

Evan said, "I have to protect myself."

Al grinned and nodded. "An increase in intelligence is his reward," he said, and then, "Anyway, you must be getting sleepy. It's late. You can sleep here tonight and in the morning we can take you wherever you want to go. How's that sound?"

Evan looked into the empty bowl and then he glanced at Kinny beside him and back at Al. The two men seemed to be watching him with a combined focus, as if they were either side of the same pair of eyes.

"Can I have some more stew?" Evan asked.

"I don't know, *can* you?" Al shot back.

Kinny squeaked and the boy looked at him and the small, doggish man had his hand cupped over his giggling mouth. His eyes were waxy.

Evan looked back at Al. He said, "*May* I have some more?"

Al's clear blue eyes smiled. "Of course," he said. "Kinny, go tell Mother Maeve she can come out for dinner now. Then we should all get to bed. It's almost midnight. This was a very special day."

CHAPTER ELEVEN

At the renewed sound of the dogs' baying, Rook turned around in the snow. As he watched, he saw the lead dog appear at the top of the hill above the glade and stop silhouetted in the low glare of the police flashlights, its breath expelling in billows. Two other dogs joined the first. Together they gathered on the hill and howled. Rook grimaced. He generally liked dogs.

He turned from the sight of his pursuers and leaned over his trapped leg and felt for the grounding chain. It was buried deep below the snow in a frozen covering of leaves. When his fingers caught the chain he pulled it up and yanked hard and the chain fed straight way to the grounding spike. He sat forward and pulled his free leg up so he was crouched over the trap.

Behind him, the dogs howled and yipped and whined, holding at the top of the hill. The yellow beams of light bounced side to side through the canopy and Rook heard the officers calling out, heard the clamour of their running on the hill. Then the yellow lights swung down and the snow all around Rook turned crystalline.

Rook reached forward and gripped the grounding spike with both hands and leaned back, pulling with all his weight. The spike tore out of the ground, taking with it a large chunk of frozen earth. Quickly, Rook wedged his free foot down and stood with the grounding chain and spike in hand.

From the top of the hill, an officer yelled, "Hey, you down there! Don't move!"

With the lights at his back, Rook heard the officers' shuffling, sliding footsteps as they descended the hill, trying not to slip. For a moment, the lights fell away from him. The cops were no doubt illuminating the paths of their own feet. Rook felt the embrace of shadow over his shoulders like a warm blanket, a cloak falling over his head. He took off at a run down the length of the frozen creek, as fast as he could manage on his hobbled foot.

Shouts echoed behind him. A gun fired and a bullet whizzed past Rook's head, the sound of the shot tearing up through the woods. The dogs bayed loudly.

Rook ducked towards the ground and then turned out of the creek bed. He lumbered up the hill, hands first in the snow, clambering like an animal. His trapped foot lagged lamely behind him. A second shot went off.

Halfway up, he paused on the slope and squatted to look back. There were six officers down in the glade and they looked small from his vantage. Their lights swung side to side in an almost comical manner, covering the course of Rook's escape along the creek.

Ahead of the officers, the dogs pulled hard against their leashes and collars. The lead dog was strained forward, dragging its handler behind, and driving its face through the snow in a zigzag pattern. Then it caught wind of something and started up onto the slope. Its handler and another officer followed.

Rook watched them. They were ascending the hill at least ten metres back from where he sat. The other four cops remained in the glade scouting the creek.

Rook took a deep breath. His right leg was going numb below the knee, and there was blood in the snow around his foot. The trap was a good twenty pounds dragging on him. He couldn't run anymore.

He was still holding the grounding chain and the long iron spike, clumped with dirt and snow, but what he was going to do with them he had little idea. He shifted his weight. Some of the dirt from the spike broke loose and fell into the snow around his foot, into his blood. An idea came to him.

The lead dog was halfway up the hill, almost parallel to Rook along the slope. Rook pulled up his right leg and started to the top of the hill at a low crouch.

At the crest of the hill, the ground flattened upon a snow-swept clearing before the copse of spruce trees. There was a strong wind blowing from the east and it would carry Rook's scent straight to the dogs.

He broke loose the rest of the clumped dirt from the spike and packed it into a ball, then rolled it in the bloodstained snow around his foot. For good measure, he squeezed the trap hard on his ankle, repressing a cry of pain, so that his blood would run fresh again. He mixed the dirt, snow, and fresh blood together in his hands, and then looked up past the trees and called to the night.

The night rushed into him instantly, as if it had been waiting. His heart jackhammered in his chest. His eyes sharpened into obsidian voids.

He dug a shallow pocket in the snow and placed his mixture in and covered it. Then he crept across the clearing towards the spruce trees. When he reached the edge of the trees he stopped and pulled in his leg and placed his hand flat on the ground. The snow melted at his touch. What he was about to do would likely draw wider, unwanted attention, but he could think of no other option.

Two beams of light swung over the top of the hill and then the lead dog appeared. Its leash was a straight black line shooting back from its neck, and its handler came up at the other end of the leash. The second officer followed. Their lights searched the clearing.

"Rise and take form, shadow," Rook whispered.

The wind rushed over his shoulder, but he felt nothing of it. His senses were tuned to the heat and current running fast through him, down his arm, into his hand where it steamed in the snow, and into the ground.

From the spot where he had buried his blood and the dirt of the earth, a dark shape emerged. At first little more than a cloud, its constitution quickly thickened until it resembled a man much the size and stature of Rook, standing plainly in the clearing. The wind blew.

The lead dog raised its head and barked and leapt forward. The two officers turned and spotted the figure in the clearing.

"Now run," Rook said.

Rook's shadowed duplicate took off across the clearing. It reached the crest of the hill and continued running, vanishing from Rook's vantage point. The lead dog and the two cops rushed down the hill after it. Rook let out his breath.

He didn't know how long his conjuring would carry his scent, but it would give the dogs a good hunt through the night. He hoped it would tie them up until morning. Of course, there was now the possibility that something other than the police would come looking for him, but he tried not to think about that. He still had more immediate problems.

Easing up on his foot, Rook tried to stand but thought better of it. He crawled under the low branches of the spruce trees instead and gathered himself on the other side. With a groan, he stretched his right leg out flat in the snow and leaned over his knee and reached for the two springs of the trap. As he leaned forward he winced. He drew a breath. He steadied himself. He gripped the metal springs one in each hand. Then he closed his hands hard and squeezed. He gritted his teeth against it and his hands shook, cold and white-knuckled, and the cutting pain shot up his leg into his lower back.

Slowly, the bowed metal bands began to close. He squeezed them together harder. As the trap opened, Rook felt the teeth coming out from the flesh of his ankle. He wiggled his foot side to side and moved the trap away, still gripping the springs. Then he pulled his foot out fast and dropped the springs and the trap snapped closed in the snow.

Rook fell back. He lay with his leg outstretched and free, staring up into the spruce canopy. His foot was numb. He could feel the night moving through the rest of his body. He sat up and cupped his hands over his mouth and began to breathe in and out against his palms. It took longer than usual, but then smoke escaped between his fingers. A small flame.

Chapter Twelve

Evan woke in a fetal position on a frozen, jagged floor, and at first the distance between dream and waking was hard to cross. He came from a faraway feeling of flowing ice and drifting snow into a sudden, shocking sense of his cold, naked, shivering body. He opened and closed his eyes. A deep impenetrable dark surrounded him, the dark of nowhere and nothing.

In a panic, he sat up and tucked in his legs. The jagged floor scraped his skin, and it felt like he was lying on a metal grate. From beyond, the dark rattled and clanged.

He stuck out his hand and his palm hit a lattice of cold steel. His fingers went through the spaces and grasped it like chain link. The tang of rusted metal came under his nose but even more overwhelming in the air was a rotten stink of death and sodden earth.

He swivelled and in doing so felt his toes scrape against cold lattice behind him. He stuck his hand to his right and felt the steel links and reached to his left where his fingers grasped the same. He put his hands up above his head and they extended in a cramped arc over him before encountering the steel roof of the confinement. He was trapped in a cage.

His heartbeat stopped, or so it felt. Then it started again at a feverish pace. He scrambled. Having swivelled around he had forgotten which way was forward, which way he had been facing when he woke. He felt, trembling, for the nearest wall of the cage and shimmied against it and gripped the links with both hands. He pressed his face against his knuckles like a prisoner peering from behind the bars of his cell into the pitch dark.

For some time, Evan sat still against the edge of the cage. Slowly he began to shiver in the cold. Then he shook harder—his entire body gave way to a violent convulsion and he screamed and slammed his body into the wall of the cage. He rocked back and slammed again, screaming, scraping his shoulder against the jagged steel. Blood ran down his arm.

His energy wore out fast. Weary and hurting, he hung limp against the cage with his fingers gripping the links. His breathing came as a long, crippling whine. He closed his eyes.

The cold sodden stink of the dark clouded around him and he felt numb. It was as if the darkness was inside his head, blotting out all else and leaving him empty. And yet, with a small sense of surprise and pride, he noticed that he was not crying.

It was then Evan heard a voice. His eyes flew open and he lifted his head. The dark rose before him like a blank wall. He saw nothing.

Then he heard the sound again and for a moment he thought it was the hiss of a snake. He drew up his legs and sat with his arms wrapped around his knees. He waited.

The strange sound came again.

Sss . . .

It was faint, but Evan was sure now that it was a voice.

"Hello?" he called.

Sss . . .

"Who's there?"

At that moment, the darkness split open and Evan ducked his head and covered his eyes from an almost blinding light. He heard the stomp of feet coming down a short set of steps. When he peered from under his arm he saw there had been a door opened from above and a tawny light spread within the room, defining the walls and floor. A man had come down and was lumbering back and forth, his path sloppy. The stinging smell of liquor moved with him, mixing with the chamber's foul rot. It was Al. Evan could see the man's green gown hanging past his knees as he staggered around the space.

It was a dirt-dug chamber with rough pinewood boards framed against the walls to keep the earth at bay. Evan saw now the fine steel links of the cage in which he was trapped. The links were rusted and stained. The cage had double-pinned locks on the front gate.

Around the perimeter of the room there were other cages. He counted six of them, each also rusted and jagged-looking. In the centre of the chamber, there was a cylindrical construction of stones, but Evan was at a loss as to what it was.

Most of the cages appeared to be empty, but not all. When Evan saw the first pair of eyes he shrank away in fear, but he crept forward again after a moment and looked.

There were two other kids, each in a separate cage. Evan was unsure whether they were girls or boys but they seemed about his age. Their hair looked long and dark and matted, and their faces were small and dirt-smeared. Only their eyes were bright. A glossy luminance as if the tawny light was bouncing from them before it could enter. An expression of sheer hopelessness was echoed on both of their faces. Evan wondered how long they had been down here.

All of a sudden, a shadow shifted past Evan's cage and Al crouched in front of him and stuck his bowl-shaped face up against the links. Evan drew back.

Al peered into the cage, as might a spectator at a zoo. "Hey," he said. "Don't be scared." His breath was rancid, his face haggard, plastered with drunken sweat. He rubbed his forefinger and thumb together, making a soft clicking sound with his tongue against his teeth. "Hey, little guy," he said. "Come on, don't be scared. How do you like your new home?"

"Let me out," Evan said.

Al laughed. Then he steadied his gaze and looked straight at Evan. "I don't like when you bark," he said. "It won't do you any good."

Evan screamed. "Let me out!"

Al lunged at the cage and grabbed both sides with his hands. His thick fingers wrapped through the links.

"No!" he yelled. "I caught you. By my blood, it's what I was destined to do. You're not going anywhere."

Evan stared out at the man and his eyes burned with a rusty colour as a wave of fury overtook his terror for a moment. Al registered Evan's eyes with a slight tilt of his head. Then he drunkenly wiped his mouth.

"We have the power to be gods," Al said. "But we live like animals." He levelled his thick finger at Evan and said, "*You* are an animal and animals need to be controlled. When an animal species gets out of control, you know what happens? It gets culled. Intelligent forces come into play. But you don't kill the adults. No. Killing adults isn't going to solve the problem. Instead, you have to kill the young."

Al stood and crossed the room. His walk was crooked, bent forward and turned back to keep his eyes trained on Evan's. He stopped in front of one of the other cages. The child inside squirmed to the back and the cage rattled.

Al knelt and looked back at Evan again. "This is a great work," he said. "One to save the human being. Pure almighty human intelligence will become again, and we will reclaim this place. You, I think, will come to understand. Maybe you will even help. Like you said, you're special. But not all of these little beasts are special like you. No. Most of them are just animals. Most of them are dead already."

Al turned and pulled up the pins of the gate and opened the cage and reached in. Right away, the child started screaming. Evan shrank away from the sound, but still he heard the cage rattling and the child screaming and crying and kicking and then he glanced up and saw Al dragging the naked, squirming child out by the ankles.

Evan shut his eyes. He cupped his hands over his ears to shut out the awful noises. Al stomped up the wooden staircase. The door closed with a thud and hushed the chamber back into darkness, but still Evan could hear the screaming.

He sat cupping his ears. The cries shot out in bursts, burning horrible images into Evan's vision in the dark.

When the screams finally stopped, there was another sound that was somehow equally as horrible. Silence. A raw, unbearable silence, in the cold, in the dark.

CHAPTER THIRTEEN

Whatever length of time passed, Evan had no real way of knowing but for the slowly calming measure of his breath. The cold dark enveloped him and he shivered. His earlier sleep had been short and given him no rest. He felt the pull of his fatigue, and yet he had never in his life been more awake and alert. He sat with his eyes open, his arms wrapped around his knees, watching every tiny shift and ripple in the blackness.

When the door opened again and the tawny light cut through the dark, it was not Al who entered but the young girl, Maeve. Her footsteps sounded on the wooden stair. Evan saw her shadow first, long and thin. Then the girl appeared in the light. In her arms she carried the child, lengthwise as she might have carried a bundle of firewood. The child's pale limbs hung limp.

She crossed to the centre of the chamber and stood before the stonework construction. Evan still could not figure out what the stone formation was, but the way the girl stood in front of it made him think of churches and candles. A crude altar.

The girl leaned over the stonework, holding out the child's body. Evan watched her. She lowered her arms, her head bowed, and then in a swift and graceful motion, she dropped the child's body and it disappeared from sight.

Evan's mouth fell open, as he realized the truth of the stonework structure. It was the mouth of a deep pit.

There had been a faint whoosh and the tumble of the body falling, and then nothing. No thud or splash when it hit the bottom. No echo. Nothing at all.

The girl turned and Evan saw her face in the light. It was wet. The jagged scar across her nose was livid and her small eyes sparkling with tears.

As she crossed in front of his cage, Evan asked, "Why are you doing this?"

The girl stopped short and turned her head, searching at first, as if ignorant of Evan and his cage. Then she saw him and their eyes met and locked.

The girl said nothing. She had a shocked, almost petrified look on her face. Evan wanted her to speak. He wanted her to tell him *why* this was happening. He remembered her name and said it in his head: *Maeve, Maeve, Maeve . . . why are you doing this?*

. . . I was his first, she said.

As if against his will, Evan slid up to the gate of his cage. He had heard Maeve's voice, but not in his ears. She had spoken right inside his head. He could feel Maeve's voice moving through him like a small snake slithering up his spine. It was a discomforting sensation. Maeve's voice—small, terrified, alone—was being drawn to Evan in his special-thinking way.

I hear you, he said in his head.

Maeve's lips were still, but her voice came clearly.

. . . I was the first he ever took. He said I was unique. He said I was blessed. He said I was destined to help save the human being. He never meant to hurt me. I was the first he saved.

The girl's eyes narrowed as she felt a faint tingling go up her spine. A warm sensation popped and spread across the left side of her brain.

As a little girl she had gone to play by the river. . . .

I remember the willow trees looked like old witches washing their long hair in the water. They had just cut the grass and it was damp and the loose bits of grass clung to my ankles and in between my toes. There was a hill that went down to the river. All across the water, these little bugs skated making ripples. . . .

Her voice went away and Evan felt a quiet weeping. Then her voice returned.

. . . Obey him. Be helpful. Give him everything. . . .

He told me I had to go with him. My mom was worried and she'd asked him to come get me. He'd take me home. He told me to get in the car.

He can show mercy. One day we are going to die.

Maeve stood still in front of Evan's cage and stared down into his rust-tinted eyes and then she blinked and shook her head. She looked at the ground as if she had lost something and then she straightened and turned away, crossing the room through the light. She went up the wooden steps and pulled the door closed with a slam.

Evan squatted in the dark. His body was humming and he had a strange, sour taste in his mouth. The girl's voice lingered in his head, in his whole body, as if flowing in his blood, gathering and revolving in his chest. He wriggled with the discomfort of it but there was no getting away. It felt like someone was digging a hole in him.

He buried his face in his hands. But where a feeling—a compulsion—to cry had once lived in him, there now existed a stark solemnity. He was reminded of the song he had heard in the cave and he cringed and wriggled to get away from the hollowing pain. He saw Rook's face in the dark and he wanted to scream.

At that moment Evan heard another voice speak.

"Hello?" it called.

Evan lifted his head. He sniffled and listened, doubtful, suspicious.

"Are you there?" the voice asked.

Evan felt his own voice come up like a tremor. He said, "I'm here."

There was silence. Evan waited. He had heard the voice in the air, in his ears, a real speaking voice. One of the other kids. It had to be real.

A cage rattled. "You can't talk to them," the voice said. "It's not allowed. They're going to come for you now."

Evan said nothing. His heart started to race. Rather than fear, the warning had filled him with excitement. An impatient rush. Thoughts of escape.

"Did you hear me?" the child asked.

"I think I can get us out of here," Evan said.

Silence. Then, "You shouldn't have talked to her. She'll tell about it. She always tells. They're going to hurt you for it. To train you. Just do whatever they say."

Evan heard footsteps thump across the floor above. He was breathing fast, the cold air like a strange ignition, and he was wondering how long it would be before they came for him. Every moment felt so long in the dark. He wished he could see the other child who spoke to him.

"What's your name?" Evan said.

The child refused to answer. Doubt flooded Evan's senses, and he wondered if there had even been a child speaking at all.

The door swung open and the tawny light cut across the dirt floor of the chamber.

Evan looked out to see who was coming down the stairs. The steps were slow and soft on the boards. He huddled against the gate of his cage and took a deep breath.

After a moment, he saw the frail, feeble legs of the one called Kinny emerge at the bottom of the stairs. His small, pigeon-toed feet staggered into the chamber. Evan closed his eyes.

Okay, you can do this.

He said the man's name in his head, *Kinny*, and he said it again, thinking *Kinny, Kinny, Kinny* . . .

He heard Kinny's slow steps drag across the dirt floor, heard him wheezing and sniffling. It went around in a circle and then crossed to Evan's side of the chamber. Then Evan's cage rattled. He heard Kinny groan as he bent down. His knees cracked. The cage rattled again.

This is it.

When Evan opened his eyes, Kinny was kneeling in front of his cage. The man's patchy-bearded face was eye-level with Evan. He was grinning, his top lip peeling back above his gums.

Evan looked right back. He stared straight into Kinny's green, murky eyes, thinking *Kinny, Kinny, Kinny* . . .

And then it seemed as if someone had taken a pair of scissors and cut some invisible stitching from Kinny's vocal chords, threads that had bound him to silence for a long time, and Evan heard the man's inner voice pour out. Broken and tormented, Kinny's words erupted in Evan's head with heavy sobs.

I'm so sorry, Kinny blubbered.

Evan listened. He felt Kinny's voice slide along his spine and he followed it, figuring it out, trying to speak back.

I'm so, so sorry. Kinny's voice poured out. *He made me do it. He always makes me do it. I can't stop him. . . . I don't know how. . . .*

The sense of Kinny's voice, his fear and pain, swirled in Evan like a rotten stench and it made him gag. He nearly vomited what little he had in his stomach onto the floor of his cage. But he kept his eyes locked on Kinny's and listened and followed the man's voice as it slithered through him and then he caught it and he answered.

He spoke slowly at first: *Kinny. Kinny, listen to me. It's okay.*

. . . I wish I could stop him. . . . I wish I could make it stop. . . . I want to go back with Miss Tolson. . . . I want to go back. . . .

It's okay, Kinny. . . .

But the man's horrid, pained voice flooded out. *She was so nice to me. She didn't make me do the bad things. She was nice. She let me peel the apples in the fall time. I could do them really good in one long peel, round and round. And she'd let me peel one extra and I got to eat it when I was done. It was fuzzy without the skin and it went all brown, but I liked the brown parts the most. Miss Tolson was nice to me. . . .*

When she died I didn't know what I . . . Then Al said I could come with him. I could help him. I didn't know how to stop it. . . .

Kinny, listen to me. It's okay now. You can help make it stop. Now's your chance to make it all better. I want you to open my cage and let me out.

I'm so, so sorry. . . .

Open my cage, Kinny. Now.

Kinny's hands rose to the double-pinned lock and pulled the topmost pin and then his hands lowered mechanically and he pulled up the second. The door of the cage gave way with a pop.

Good, Kinny. You're helping. Now go stand in the corner.

I'm so sorry.

Go. Don't come out until I tell you.

Kinny stood and turned and walked with his arms flat at his sides straight to the corner of the chamber between two empty cages and faced the pinewood boarding. Evan waited and then pushed open the cage door and crawled out. The dirt floor was cold but it felt alive and fresh and he was glad to touch it. He looked up the stairs in the light. The door was open. He couldn't see much of the room above, didn't know where it would lead him, but he wasn't going to give up.

You can get out of here.

He squatted at the edge of his cage for a moment longer and waited. The creak of a chair and other vague noises carried from the floor above, but it was mostly quiet. He crawled farther into the chamber.

Straight ahead of him was the stonework pit. Evan skirted it and crawled across the ground to the other side of the chamber. He passed an empty cage, then came to another and stopped. Inside was the child that had spoken to him. A red-haired boy about Evan's age.

Evan glanced once at Kinny, who stood still in the corner as commanded, then back to the boy. He put his finger over his lips. The red-haired boy sat on his haunches with his knees up. Evan could smell him but he tried to ignore it as he felt along the frame of the cage for the pins. He drew up the first. It made a dull ping sound.

Evan stopped and looked over his shoulder and waited. Footsteps creaked from above. Nothing crossed in the light of the doorway. He turned back to the cage and reached to the second pin and started pulling it up—

Sss . . .

Evan turned around fast. He looked to the corner, but Kinny stood as before. Evan looked around the rest of the shadowy chamber. There was nothing else there.

The boy in the cage shifted and the cage rattled and Evan turned back. He looked in at the boy and they nodded to each other. Evan reached back to the second pin and started again. Then he stopped once more and glanced over his shoulder. A low, whispering hiss rolled towards him.

Sss . . .

Evan turned his back to the cage, leaving the final pin still locked. The boy inside rattled the gate, but Evan ignored him. He moved in search of the sound, drawn by a will not his own, drawn by a knowledge that what he heard was a voice.

"Where are you going?" the other boy whispered.

Evan knew he should turn back. He should pull up the final pin and let the boy out. He knew it. Go back, he told himself. *Stop!*

But he moved as if by a power beyond him. Like curiosity coupled with an innate sense of return, blind and mindless as the last few steps taken when arriving home. The voice called to him.

Sss . . . Sss . . . Sss . . .

It led him to the stonework at the centre of the chamber. When he reached it he placed his palms flat on the cold stone rim and leaned over the mouth and looked down into the dark hollow pit.

The sound rose up from below, and Evan heard many tongues speaking at once. He could feel them reaching along his spine, like the voices of Maeve and Kinny. They pleaded.

Such suffering . . . he butchered us and left us to rot . . . avenge us . . .

Entranced by the voices, Evan did not notice the shadow that cut through the light on the stairs. He didn't hear the heavy tread on the wood boards, and he didn't hear Al's rasping breath until it was too late.

"What the fucking hell do you thinking you're doing?"

Evan turned around as Al's fist cracked against the side of his head and he landed flat on his stomach in the dirt. Bleary-eyed, he saw Al's bare feet stomp before his face. A sweaty hand gripped the back of his neck and he was yanked to his feet, trying hard not to scream.

Chapter Fourteen

Rook wasted no time after freeing his foot from the trap and cauterizing the wound with the flame he had conjured, but still he walked with a limp. He picked up a set of tracks in the snow through the woods and followed them to the edge of the trees where they vanished below the sweep of a broad clearing. There had been three sets of tracks, two large enough to be the footprints of men and one set much smaller and closer-spaced that Rook believed to be Evan's.

Standing at the border of the clearing, he estimated their path. A fresh snow had started to fall over the clearing. Large white flakes whirled in the wind and the field looked like a sandy white beach smoothed by the roll of waves. Behind him the trees swayed and creaked in the grey dark. It must have been about midnight. He had not heard or smelled any sign of the police or the dogs. He had time.

He squatted near the last trace of the tracks and aligned his eye with even the slightest marks or indentations in the snow. He squinted against the slanting wind and scratched through his beard to his chin. His right calf was still numb and it felt like he was squatting on one leg. But at least he was no longer bleeding. He closed his eyes and tried to listen.

"Where are you?" he muttered.

He breathed calmly. The wind whipped past his ears and rolled away and came back. The woods rustled. The highway hummed far in the distance. And then he heard the first beat. It was distant, but he heard another. He focused, cutting away the wind and the sway of the trees, and then he heard the child's heartbeat clearly.

It was racing.

Rook stood stiffly and started across the clearing.

He followed the beat in his head until he spotted the dark shape of a cabin in the distance. Glancing down, he discovered shallow dips in the snow. He stepped back. The tracks were half-buried but he found three sets as before, one set much smaller than the others. Aligning his eye to their course, he saw that they curved and vanished and reappeared, all three leading straight to the cabin. He took off at a limping run.

When Rook reached the cabin, he approached around its western wall looking for the door. The racing beat in his head had grown louder. He knew Evan was inside.

The cabin's windows were crudely shuttered, nails sticking out through the slats, but slivers of the inner light escaped along the frame. A chimney pipe smoked from the roof, and Rook followed the billowing trail around the other side of the cabin. He spotted a white passenger van parked under a tree, and another car buried in snow.

The door to the cabin was sheltered under a blue tarpaulin billowing in the wind. As he reached it, he heard a scream. Whether it was real above the wind or connected to the heartbeat he followed in his head, he couldn't tell.

The door was locked and so Rook kicked it in. The force of it shuddered up his leg, and he almost dropped to a knee, but a rush of adrenalin kept him going. With a crash, the door had hit the adjoining wall.

Rook stepped over the threshold. The stifled air of the cabin reeked with festering rot and the metallic saline of blood.

In the centre of the room there was a table, and a young girl stood at its edge holding a tin pail. She stared at Rook with a shocked, guilty expression. Behind the table, a large man whose bare chest was matted with brown hair and spotted with blood stood panting. A brief look of surprise swept over his concave face like light glimmering through a bowl. A third person stood off to Rook's right side in the corner of the cabin. He was a small and feeble-looking man, wide-eyed and hesitant.

Rook saw these three people and saw them only. He knew in his heart that Evan was here. Standing in the doorway, Rook drew the night in around him. His eyes turned black as the space between stars, and the cabin darkened. Like animals, everyone in the cabin could sense the predator in Rook. The girl froze. The big man squared his shoulders. A dark patch spilled down the feeble man's left leg. Then Rook started for them.

The girl turned and fled through a curtain into another room. Her tin pail clanged to the floor.

Rook went for the larger man first. As he passed the stovetop, in one smooth motion he picked up a cast-iron skillet that was steaming and swung it sideways at the feeble man behind him. The man screamed and fell to his knees, clutching his face. Rook continued forward without pause.

The bare-chested man had picked up an iron poker. When he swung, the poker smacked flat against Rook's open palm and his fingers closed around it. Rook stepped once and picked up a clear glass jug from the table and smashed it over the man's head. He pulled the poker free and whipped the man across his knees, dropping him. Rook struck him across the face with the poker and then tossed it across the room.

Right then, the girl ran back out of the other room. Rook caught her by the shoulders, but not before she drove a knife into Rook's abdomen. He growled and pushed her back and then punched her in the face. She fell into the doorway, tearing down the curtain, and lay on the floor between the two rooms.

Rook groaned and placed his hand on the knife handle sticking from him. He started to pull it out, but decided against it. From the corner of the room, the scalded man lay curled and whimpering. The big bare-chested man lay on the floor, his face a bloodied, pulped mess. Rook stepped over the girl and went into the next room.

There were two beds and Rook pulled back the blankets and turned over the mattresses. He knelt and looked under the wood bunks. He stood. He called out Evan's name.

Nothing.

Rook went back to the main room, stepping over the girl, and knelt beside the table. The bare-chested man had turned over on his stomach and Rook rolled him back.

"Where is the boy?" Rook asked.

The man wheezed, his bloodied face beginning to swell.

Rook grabbed a piece of shattered glass and pressed it into the man's right ear. A sharp cry pierced the silence of the cabin.

"Tell me where he is!"

The man raised his arm and pointed into the second room.

"Where?" Rook asked again.

"In the cellar. There's a door in the wall."

Rook stood and went again into the second room. There was a sheet pinned to the wall across from the beds. He tore it down and there was indeed a small door hidden under it. He snapped back the latch and pulled it open. The smell hit him and Rook put his arm over his nose and mouth. In the meagre light he saw a short staircase leading down into near total darkness.

Ducking his head, he went down the stairs. He froze when he saw the cages, the full reality of this place dawning on him at once.

In the cage nearest the stairs he saw Evan, and the sight made his chest heave.

Evan lay curled and naked with his wrists and ankles bound together behind his back. A leather muzzle was buckled onto his face. His rust-coloured eyes were bright and when he saw Rook, they ran with tears.

Rook opened the cage and pulled Evan out gently. He carried him up the stairs and placed him on the bed and removed the muzzle from his face. Evan gasped. Rook untied his wrists and ankles and Evan curled into himself.

Rook covered Evan with a blanket. He looked around the room for clothes. A pair of dirty socks hung over one of the bunk posts. Rook grabbed the socks and fished for Evan's little feet under the blanket and fitted the socks over his toes and pulled them up his ankles.

"Rook . . ." Evan said.

Underneath one of the beds Rook found a garbage bag filled with clothes. The articles varied in size and condition but they were all children's clothes. There must have been a dozen or more pairs of pants. Rook dug out underwear and a pair of jeans and a T-shirt and sweater and he dressed Evan, kneeling in front of him. He found Evan's boots and his oversized peacoat, strapped the boots and buttoned the coat.

"Rook," Evan said. "I thought you were dead."

"Well, I'm not. We have to go."

"Wait," Evan said. "Down there. We have to let him out."

Rook glanced over his shoulder to the small open doorway and the dark staircase. He turned back to Evan.

"There's someone else down there?" he asked.

Evan nodded. "Another little boy."

Evan got off the bed and walked to the doorway. He waited for Rook to follow him and they went down.

In the cellar, Evan crossed to boy's cage and pulled up the second pin and the door popped open. Evan looked in and saw the boy sitting cramped at the back.

"Hey," Evan said. "You can come out now, it's okay."

The boy shook his head.

Evan beckoned to him. "We're safe," Evan said. "Trust me."

The child shuffled forward. Evan glanced back at Rook and saw him looking down into the stonework pit.

"They put the bodies down there," Evan said.

Rook glanced at Evan, then looked down into the pit again. He grabbed hold of its stonework edge which cracked under his grip. His whole body shook with suppressed violence, as though the truth of what lay in those depths had been revealed to him alone. Then all at once he wrenched himself away and stormed up the stairs.

Evan called after him, but Rook didn't answer. The sounds of his heavy feet on the floor above made the newly freed child recoil back into his cage.

Evan turned to him. "It's okay," he said. "He's on our side. Come on out."

Then they heard Rook's stomping again. He sounded much heavier. Across the two rooms and coming down the stairs. When Rook emerged in the chamber with the light at his back, his silhouette looked like some huge, hulking monster. He had the man, Al, slung over his shoulder.

"What are you doing?" Evan said in alarm.

Rook said nothing. He stepped to the edge of the pit and swung Al off his shoulder and laid him out across the mouth of the stonework. Al gasped and tried to sit up but Rook placed a hand on Al's chest and then punched him in the face.

Al's head reeled back. He coughed and choked with blood. Then he started to laugh.

"Go ahead," Al muttered. "Send me down. Send me to be with those I saved. Let me go to them. Let me be saved, too. Go on. Do it."

Rook glared at him. "You're going to Hell," he said.

Again, Al let out a choked laugh. Rook punched him again. Then he grabbed Al's legs and folded them up towards his chest and started to cram the man down into the pit.

"Yes," Al said. "Send me to them. Send me down!"

"No," Evan shouted, running over to Rook and grabbing his arm. "Stop it!"

Rook shook Evan off. "This has nothing to do with you!"

"You can't kill him. You have to leave him for the cops."

Rook let up and held Al still.

"He wants you to kill him," Evan said.

"Good. He deserves to die."

"But it's better if we leave him for the cops. That's what he's scared of."

Rook fumed but relented. He lifted Al back up and dumped him on the floor.

"It's better this way," Evan said. "Let the cops get him."

Rook said nothing. He turned away and rubbed his face with both hands as once again a kind of rigid violence went through him.

Seated on the dirt floor with his back against the stonework pit, Al let out a slight sigh of relief. He pushed the blood around in his mouth with his tongue and then spat and wiped some blood from his face. Then he laughed again.

He said, "Oh, I'm not scared of going to Hell. You think you've been there? Well let me tell you, I'm there all the time."

Evan glared at him. "Shut up," he said. "Just stop talking."

Al rolled his gaze to Evan. "Oh, how the little beast barks. Bark, bark, bark! This is the real hell, among these animals, pretending."

Evan saw Rook's fists clench several times, his whole body rigid. "And that's why I had to do it," Al said. "And I'll do it again."

Slowly, Rook turned around. He stared down at the man on the floor. Then he lowered to a knee beside him. He looked at the dirt around his feet, as if considering its chemistry. Evan watched him and wished Rook would stand up and walk away, but he said nothing this time. He waited.

Al started to say something, but all at once Rook grabbed his head with his whole hand and smashed it against the side of the stonework until it came apart like a big red egg. He hooked his hands under Al's armpits and hoisted him up to a seated position on the edge of the stone, then shoved him backwards into the pit. He slid a ways and finally dropped.

There was a slight whoosh sound. Rook glanced at Evan and then turned and walked to the staircase.

"Don't take long," he said over his shoulder.

Rook went upstairs and found that the girl was no longer lying on the floor between the two rooms. The feeble man whom he had scalded was also gone. He stepped outside and saw their tracks leading away to the trees beyond the vehicles. With a swift yank, he pulled the girl's knife from his side and tossed it into the snow. Warm blood ran down his thigh. He placed his hand over the wound and once more looked up into the night sky, but drew nothing to him. He couldn't muster the call. His eyes closed and his shoulder slumped. He wanted to sit down. He went back inside to find something to keep pressure on his wound.

— •

Evan came up the stairs with the red-haired boy following him. Rook stood in the doorway between the two upper rooms. He had a blanket in his hands. When the red-haired boy saw Rook, he almost screamed.

"It's okay," Evan said. "He won't hurt you."

Rook handed the blanket to Evan, who gave it to the other boy and helped him wrap himself. Then they found him some clothes and helped him dress. The boy sat down on the bed.

Rook looked at Evan and said, "Tell him to stay right there. The police should find this place by the time the sun comes up."

"I want to stay with him," Evan said.

"We're not staying."

Evan said nothing. He looked only at the red-haired boy. Then he said, "Okay, just stay here. The police are coming. They'll find you."

The boy stared at Evan. He pulled the blanket closer to his chin.

"Let's go," Rook said.

Evan refused to answer.

"Now."

When they left, Evan turned and gave the boy a last look before he and Rook walked out the front door. Outside, they heard the sound of sirens rising over the woods.

CHAPTER FIFTEEN

Rook had found the keys to the white passenger van hanging on a nail, and he lifted Evan into his seat and then got in on the driver's side. Evan sat with his hands in his lap. The van was cold and the darkness seemed to press against the glass.

"Why can't we take that boy with us?" Evan said.

"Because we can't. He'll be better off if he waits here for the police."

"But I wouldn't be, would I?"

Rook slid the key in the ignition. "No," he said. "We have to keep going."

"You mean keep running," Evan said.

Rook said nothing. The engine started and the dashboard lit up. The digital clock read: 1:42 a.m. The gas light came on, the tank sitting on empty.

Better than nothing, Rook thought. He switched on the headlights.

The red-haired boy was standing out in front of the van. His eyes were gone, burned-out to blackened holes. It made his face looked shadowed even in the glare of the headlights, but Rook and Evan recognized the dreadful sight right away. It was the same thing they had seen on the bus.

Evan screamed. "Rook, out there!"

"I see it. Hold on."

Rook pulled the transmission arm into drive and put his foot on the gas and the van drove forward. The thing that had been the red-haired boy lunged into the front of the van, then disappeared underneath. They felt the body bump below their seats. Rook didn't stop. He swung the van around and drove northeast away from the cabin towards a gap he had spotted in the trees.

They sped through a narrow lane of tall grey pines and then the trees fell away and there were only barren bushes of dogwood and sumac covered in snow at either side. Eventually they came to a road and Rook turned left.

It was a two-lane county road without lampposts. The darkness swept over the windows like the wisps of a passing phantom. Rook held the wheel steady and watched beyond the beam of the headlights for any obstacle. His glances to the rear-view mirror were quick and wary.

The image of the red-haired boy falling under the front of the van was stuck in his mind, and he kicked himself for having conjured a shadow to escape the police. He'd known something would sense it. That *thing* had been out there looking for them ever since the highway, and now it had found them again. He doubted that it had died with the boy. It would find another body. He tried not to think of it.

The drive was smooth.

The road met a T-intersection and Rook scanned both directions. He turned the wheel to the right and pulled forward and drove on.

Looking out the passenger window, Evan saw his face reflected in the dark glass and he hardly recognized it. Beside his own reflection, he saw Rook's shape over the steering wheel, a blurry image both foreign and familiar. The blurred reflection turned once and looked at him and then looked away. Seeing it, Evan felt the pleasure and comfort of safety. A smell of damp stone and wood smoke came to him. And yet his feelings betrayed him. A fire burned in him, raging at Rook for having come back. In some way, Rook's return made Evan feel small and weak again, even as it seemed to be a kind of blessing.

After some time, Evan turned in his seat and stared straight at Rook, wanting the man to notice him. He felt bottled up with a bunch of things he wanted to shout and scream, both angry and glad, but he wanted Rook to see it on his face. He watched Rook shift in the driver's seat to lean against the door, keeping his eyes on the road. Evan felt the silence between them grow heavy. The engine hummed and there was a faint yet persistent ticking from somewhere behind the dashboard.

Rook shifted again into the door, and he glanced once at Evan and saw his earnest stare. "What?" he asked.

"I thought I would never see you again," Evan said.

"Did they hurt you?"

Evan shook his head. "When I heard the gunshot, I thought . . . I thought they got you."

"I thought that for a moment, myself."

Evan smiled. It just came out. Inside he was angry, or he wanted to be. Rook shifted again and winced.

"What's wrong?" Evan said.

"Nothing."

"Are you hurt?"

Rook pulled himself up. "I'm fine."

Evan leaned across the middle of the van. He peered around at Rook's body as if he had a magnifying glass in his hand. At first he thought Rook was telling the truth because he could see nothing. But then he spotted the dark stain on Rook's coat and all down his thigh.

"You're bleeding," Evan said.

"Sit straight," Rook told him, edging Evan back to his seat.

Evan took hold of Rook's arm. "Who hurt you?" he asked, his small voice full of vengeance.

Rook was silent. Then he said, "The girl rushed me when I wasn't looking. She stabbed me with a damn kitchen knife."

Evan cringed. "Does it hurt bad? What are you going to do? Can you heal it, like you did with my knee?"

"I've tried. I'll try again when we stop."

After a moment, Evan said, "Did you kill her, too?"

"No. She ran off. Her and the little guy. They ought to keep running forever."

"Good."

"Good?"

Evan nodded. "Maeve and Kinny didn't deserve to die." He said their names as if they were old friends of his. "They weren't bad people."

"They were horrible people," Rook said.

"No, they weren't. They were just scared." Evan crossed his arms over his chest and looked out the window. He said, "I used my special-thinking on them."

Rook glanced at him. "You did?"

"Yep. I heard their thoughts, and they said they were sorry. They didn't want to be doing those things. They were just scared and trapped."

"Trapped or not, they were bad people."

"I don't think there's bad people anymore," Evan said. "There's no good people, either. There's just . . . people."

"I assure you, there *are* bad people. Those were bad people, and they got what they deserved."

"How do you know that?"

"I just do."

Evan sat quietly. After a moment, he said, nearly whispering, "Something bad happened to you, didn't it?"

Rook's expression hardened. "Don't go trying to get into my head."

"Don't worry," Evan said, spitefully. "It doesn't work on you. You're not scared of anything." He turned from Rook and faced the dark window, then looked back. "Rook," he said. "Do you think my special-thinking made a ripple? Is that why it came and got the boy?"

"Did you *really* listen to their thoughts?" Rook asked.

Evan nodded. "I really did. Will the monsters find us now?"

"No," Rook said. "What happened to that boy was my fault. I've felt no ripple come from you, Evan. If you really did listen to their thoughts, then your magic must be hidden."

A small smile of relief touched Evan's face. He yawned and nestled into his seat. He closed his eyes. After a moment, he said, "Rook?"

"Yes."

"Thank you."

Rook sighed, thinking of all that had happened to get them to this place. He remembered Evan's words: *There's just people.*

He wished Evan were right, and he hated that Evan was wrong. There was still the church ahead of them, and Rook's oath. There was still the deal to be done, and the return of Rook's wife, Allison.

Rook glanced at Evan and saw that he was asleep. His chest warmed at the sight. In another life, Rook could have watched Evan sleep forever.

They drove for a while longer before the van started making a dry glugging noise. The gas light had been on since they'd started driving; now the engine light came on as well. Rook eased his foot on the gas pedal and kept the van going. He had been following to the back roads, away from the highway, but they were still a half-hour drive from where he wanted to be. As he was hoping they would make it, giving the steering wheel a soft pat of encouragement, the glugging noise turned into a loud, hollow grinding. Rook took his foot off the gas. The van kicked as the engine failed. Rook steered it to a stop on the shoulder of the road.

"Okay," he said. "Okay."

Rook sat up and placed his hand on his knife wound. He pulled aside his jacket and lifted his shirt and the torn towel he had used to wrap himself and examined the thin, vertical opening. It was bleeding but the blood was thick and slow. He cupped his palm flat over the wound and eased back into the headrest and then drew a deep, slow, exhausted breath. He still lacked the energy to call the night.

Rook's eyes fell shut but he opened them right away. Evan still slept. Slowly, Rook opened his door. The cold reached him, slowing him further. He pivoted from the seated and stepped down. When he stood straight, he winced at the ripping pain in his abdomen and coughed a gush of blood up over his lips and beard.

Rook steadied himself against the open door and he coughed and hacked and spit to clear the blood from his throat. He wiped his mouth. He reached down and fed a handful of snow into his mouth and chewed it and spat it out and did it again. He rubbed his beard with more snow and wiped his mouth one final time. Then he came around the front of the van to the passenger side.

When Rook opened the door, Evan woke from the sheer shock of the cold.

"Come on," Rook said. "Get out."

Evan hopped down from his seat and rubbed his eyes. His lips started to chatter. Rook buttoned the peacoat to the top and flipped the collar to cover Evan's face.

"Is the car dead?" Evan said.

"Ran out of gas."

"What do we do now?"

"We walk. How are your feet?"

"They're okay."

"Come on."

They started down the road. The moon was a haze of yellow behind the clouds, and the landscape held that predawn stillness in which it seemed anything could happen.

Rook paused and took Evan's hand, considering their course. Evan waited.

"This way," Rook said. "Follow me."

"Back into the woods?"

"Yes. I won't let anything happen to you. I promise."

They crossed the road and entered a deep entanglement of wintered bramble. After a few steps, they reached an old wire fence forbidding trespassers and Rook stepped down on the top line, squashing the whole fence to the ground. He lifted Evan over and then stepped over himself. The fence sprang back up behind them. They walked.

They crossed a low clearing and the snow was deep. The wind was down and no sounds carried. Dormant birch trees stood along the wings like the guardians of some sacred corridor, tall and white in the looming moonlight.

Evan lifted his knees high with each step. Ahead of him, Rook walked buckled over on his right side, his arm pulled in against his flank, his steps pecking forward through the snow. Evan imagined Rook like a giant black bird, his breath lifting up above his head like wings.

Their way led up a hill and the snow was finer and harder. They had to turn their feet at outward angles to wedge steps under the ice. Evan slipped twice and slid down before catching himself. Then he stood and stepped with his right foot and dug his heel into the ice first and planted his toe, then launched his left heel into the ice and again his right until he was running. When he passed Rook, he turned and looked at him and grinned, feeling proud of his achievement. Rook trudged on after him. At the top, Evan stood gulping air.

They had reached the crest of a hill that rose above the canopy of the trees and they put their arms over their faces against the wind.

They could see down the hill through the woods and in the distance a town. Evan looked out. Snaking among the trees, there was a hidden driveway leading up through the hills to a house. It was a huge mansion, towering, and dark.

"Is that where we're going?" Evan said.

"No."

"Where are we going?"

"To a friend's house."

"You have a friend?"

Rook looked at Evan over the wind. "Yes," he said. "Her name is August. You can trust her."

Evan gawked. "And she's a *girl*?"

"How are your feet?"

"Really cold."

Over the tops of the trees the lights of the town in the distance shone. The moonlight gave an outline of buildings and a silhouetted globular water tower. Looking over the town, the glow of city lights drew from Evan a reminiscence neither resentful nor nostalgic, but rather a feeling of looking upon an old world. A world in which, somehow, he no longer truly lived. His eye was drawn to the faint glimmering of a surface of water, dark and winding below the trees.

"Look, a river!" Evan said.

Rook looked out, unimpressed.

"Where does it go?" Evan asked.

"Where all rivers go, I suppose. The ocean."

Evan nodded as if he should have known that.

"Come on, we still have a ways to go."

"How far?" Evan had assumed they were almost done.

"There's a town over these hills. Shade's Mills." Rook turned his face out of the wind, planted both hands over his side.

"You're hurt bad," Evan said. "But you said you could heal it."

"It's deeper than I thought."

"Well then we have to get going. Come on, Rook!"

Evan started along the top of the hill and then paused and waited for Rook to join him and lead the way. They came to a cluster of small poplars and there, using the bare branches as handholds, started down the opposite slope.

Evan's boots filled with snow as they descended and when he stopped at the bottom out of the wind to check them he found the rubber soles had torn open. They were shorn with ice.

Rook looked back, gasping. "What's wrong?" he called.

"You keep going," Evan said. "I'm okay. I'll catch up."

"Lift your feet."

Evan hurried after him. They crossed the snowy flat and mounted another, lower rise. At the top Evan stopped and shook his feet in the air, but ice and snow clung to him. Inside his boots, his socks were soaked and stiff and he curled his toes to fight the numbness. The cold shot up his legs. He hurried after Rook, who was already descending the other side of the hill.

● — — —

After an hour they had crossed several rises and glades and they were stiff and tired and cold. Their sweat stuck like ice to their skin and their blood pumped like some heated elixir, keeping them going. The air hurt to breathe, stinging their throats.

They descended one last hill and crossed a shallow, top-frozen stream and walked out through a final cluster of trees. At the edge of the wood they stopped and looked dismally upon the expanse of a barren, snowbound cornfield. But on the far side of the field they saw at last the moonlit outline of the town.

It was built on a hill, leading up from the river several kilometres below to the east. Evan could see the pointed roofs of houses in rows at one end and square-shaped buildings in the middle of town, and then halfway up the hill there were small, snow-roofed dwellings, dark blue in the lunar light.

"You see that one up on the hill," Rook said. He raised his hand and pointed.

Evan nodded.

"That's where we're going."

"It's still so far."

"It's closer than it ever was before."

Hunkering against the sudden gusts of wind, they started across the cornfield. Rook trudged ahead. He breathed hard and rasping. He was curled right over at the waist, with both hands pressed tight against his wound.

Behind him, Evan hobbled. The boy could not feel his feet. Only a numb sensation somewhere below his knees. He staggered against the wind. Then he stopped walking altogether.

Rook glanced back and yelled. "Come on, Evan. Don't stop."

"Rook . . . my feet."

"Come on. Lift your legs."

Evan looked down at his feet in the snow. Tears welled in his eyes. "I can't," he yelled. "I can't, Rook!"

Rook trudged back through the snow, the wind slamming into his back. When he was within arm's reach of Evan he pulled his hands from his side and a pain shot through his abdomen that made him roar and drop to one knee. Evan called out his name.

The pain flared again and Rook fell onto his side in the snow. He was below the force of the wind, breathing raggedly. The tearing, ripping pain came whenever he tried to move. From under him, a dark pool was spreading over the snow.

Evan dropped down beside him, terrified and frozen, not feeling his face, his hands, his legs, hearing only his own heartbeat in his ears. Rook thought Evan was shouting his name, but his voice seemed far away.

A gust of wind swirled up from the field and Evan ducked his head and shut his eyes. The world around him became nothing but the timeless, incensed screaming of the cold that erased everything but the thumping in his ears. Tears froze on his cheeks in the wind. His heart beat rapidly. A clear double beat.

And then a voice came to him. Evan heard it and felt it as if he himself had spoken.

"It's okay. I have you. Let me help."

When he moved it was to the double beat of his heart. He took hold of Rook's arm, pulling him up, lifting his great weight to that steady beat and call.

And again the voice came. This time Evan heard it clear in his ears. There might as well have been someone standing next to him whispering, but there wasn't. The voice was moving through Evan. It was coming out of him, speaking clearly.

"Good, Evan. Find the strength. I have you."

He slid underneath Rook, so the man was on his back. And somehow Evan was crawling. And then he was walking. Blind in the wind and oblivious to the ice splintering across his face or the weight of Rook on his back, he carried the man and himself like he was floating.

There was only his heartbeat, his heartbeat.

August Jones was not sleeping. She lay in bed with her gaze upon the high, white stucco of the ceiling, following the concentric intricacies round and round, waiting for something. She could not say what it was, only that the pull of sleep had not visited her this night and instead she lay awake, neither restless nor worried, but simply aware of some imminent occurrence for which it was wise to be awake. It reminded her of her earliest encounters with ghosts.

She sat up and reached to her nightstand for a slim, gold-trimmed case embossed with the inner workings of a clock. She opened it and slid out a cigarette, closed it, and exchanged the case on the stand for a small black lighter. The flame cast the shadow of her hands on the bed cover. Then she placed the lighter down and leaned back into the pillows and smoked.

She had started smoking when she was thirteen, in middle school. One of the older girls had made a comment that August had the jitters. August hadn't known what that meant exactly, something similar to what they called cooties, perhaps. The older girl opened her purse and presented a cigarette and told August it would help with her jitters. Oddly, it did, curing August of an ailment she had never known she possessed until they were gone.

Thinking back, her jitters had started when she was eleven years old, the night she saw the black thing come down the hallway. She had been kept awake that night, not from restlessness but rather a premonition that there was some reason to stay up. As the hours had passed, sleep pulled at her and it had become a struggle to keep her eyes open. In the daze of half-sleep, she had started to dream, but it had felt different. It was a vision. She'd seen the bathroom down the hall from her bedroom, and there had been a dark figure standing in the doorway.

She'd known she was lying in her bed, and she couldn't possibly see down the hall. But there it was before her eyes. She'd tried to stop it, to wake up, to turn over, sit up, but her body wouldn't move. The black figure in the doorway had turned towards her. It had hung in the air like a large wet shroud, dripping and evaporating into trails of black smoke. Then it had rushed down the hall towards her.

August's screams had been muted, but she had shaken madly and kicked her legs until at last she'd broke free from the grip that pinned her and she'd sat up, fully awake. Her whole body had trembled, still reeling from the final moment of the nightmare where the black thing had knelt beside her bed, its long arm reaching to cover her mouth. But that had just been a dream.

The thing that she'd seen standing clear in the lamplight of her room when she'd woken was a ghost, long and black and shivering as if trapped in a freezer. That was when her jitters began. But smoking helped.

August stamped out the cigarette in the ashtray on the nightstand. She checked the time on her cell-phone: 3:32 a.m.

Any minute now, she thought.

When she heard the knocking on the window of her front door, she got up, slid her feet into her slippers, and walked downstairs.

Outside her front door she saw the small, tear-streaked face of a young boy, and beside him on the ground an unconscious man who she knew right away was Rook.

— • •

August flung open the door.

"My god," she said. "What's happened? Is he okay?"

Evan said nothing. He started trying to drag Rook into the house. August helped him and they managed to slide him across the foyer and into the kitchen beside the wooden island. August looked at the blood on her palms. Then shook her head.

"Get his coat off," she said. "I'll be right back." She left the kitchen, her nightgown flowing behind her.

Evan knelt beside Rook and slowly raised the man's hands from where they lay rigid and ice-cold against his chest. He unbuttoned the coat but then stopped. Rook's beard was wet with melted snow and his eyes were closed. Evan thought he looked dead.

August returned to the kitchen with a pillow.

"I told you to get his coat off," she said.

Evan looked up and his eyes were rounded with tears. He sniffled.

"Oh, it's going to be all right," August said as she knelt down beside Rook, opposite the boy. "He's been through worse."

Evan wiped his eyes. August lifted Rook's head and slid the pillow underneath.

"You stupid old fool," she said, and then, "Come on, help me get his coat off."

They lifted him up onto one elbow at a time and slipped his coat off and eased him back down. Rook's shirt was stained with sweat and soaked almost black with blood along his side.

"Let me see," August said.

The cloth was stuck with ice and blood to his skin.

"Get a cup of warm water."

Evan hopped to his feet and grabbed a glass from the rack at the sink and ran the tap and stood there waiting for it to warm and looked down at Rook and wished his eyes would open. When the water turned hot he shook his hand away from the stream and filled the glass. The water looked murky and the glass was warm when he handed it to August. She poured it generously over Rook's side, loosening the cloth. Rook lay still.

When she pulled the shirt back she shuddered. Just below Rook's ribcage on the right side the slashed red flesh looked like a bloody sinkhole that sucked open with each filling of his slow breath. The surrounding skin was red and swollen and a dark bruise stretched all across his abdomen. August pulled a tea towel from the rung on the side of the kitchen island.

"It's really bad," Evan said.

"It doesn't look good, that's for sure. But he's breathing."

"What do we do?"

Evan stood over August's shoulder with his fists clenched beside his head. He stared down at the wound, unblinking.

All of a sudden, Rook reached and grabbed August's hand as she gently dabbed the wound with the cloth. She jolted and screamed. Rook's eyes opened and he looked up at her. The hardness of his expression relaxed.

Then he looked past her and saw Evan and his eyes widened with some revelation, and he seemed, for a moment, afraid. He turned his eyes back to August.

"I hope we didn't wake you," he said.

"Of course not."

"I need you to stitch me up."

"No shit," August said and shook her head. She drew a breath and pulled back her hair and wound it into a tight bun with a hair elastic from her wrist. Then to Evan, "Get some more water, I'll be right back."

Evan filled the glass again and returned. He knelt at Rook's side.

"Do you want something to bite?"

"What?"

"I saw it in a movie. A guy bit on a stick when something hurt a lot."

"I'll be fine." Rook looked at the ceiling. His mind was back in the cornfield, trying to remember what had happened, what he'd *heard*, and how he'd ended up on August's kitchen floor.

August returned with a blue and white polka-dot sewing basket and a bottle of rubbing alcohol. She knelt at Rook's side and opened the basket and removed a spool of black thread and a packet of needles and carefully threaded a two-inch needle.

"I don't really know what I'm doing," she said.

"There's a hole. Just close it up."

"I want to wash it all with the alcohol first."

Evan sat watching August's hands as she twisted the cap from the plastic bottle. The careful movements of her fingers gave him a warm, pleasing sensation all through his body. It was a pleasant distraction, but he was worried about Rook. The stab was really bad. Evan's face flushed and tingled. The sensation in him became more than pleasing. It was invigorating.

Evan's heart skipped. His breath was hot in his throat. He had an urge to run outside, to breathe in the night air. But he couldn't leave Rook. His eyes jumped fast to the window above the kitchen sink from where he thought he'd heard someone call out his name.

"Rook, I can't do this," August said.

"Yes, you can, just focus."

"No, I mean *I can't*. My hand is shaking."

Evan slid closer to Rook on his knees, and Rook looked up at him.

Evan's eyes were the colour of rust.

When Evan reached out his hand, Rook flinched away, thinking again of the cornfield, the wind blowing, and the voice that had spoken.

"It's okay, Rook," Evan said. "I'm here. Let me help."

"What are you doing?" August asked.

Evan placed his hand flat over the gash in Rook's side, pressed gently with his weight.

"Rook?" August asked, watching Evan's hand.

Rook said nothing. His whole stomach and chest had warmed the instant Evan's hand had touched him. With his head propped up on the pillow, Rook watched Evan's hand as it began to glow.

"Oh my god," August said. "What's he doing?"

They were all in awe, Evan most of all.

"Rook," August pleaded. "What's he doing?"

"He's calling the night," Rook said.

"I'm like you, Rook." The tone of triumph in Evan's voice was matched only by his own surprise.

"Yes, I see, Evan." The pain was leaving Rook, far faster than he'd ever been able to heal himself. It was like Evan's hand was a sponge. He could feel the tingling, indescribable part when flesh fuses back together. "That's good," he said. "That's enough, Evan."

Evan lifted his hand away. He was beaming, and his eyes had returned to a natural brown. Rook's wound had transformed from a deep puncture to a shallow cut.

Evan stood, then turned and went out of the kitchen into the dining room. He wobbled, as if drifting with sudden exhaustion. Rook and August watched him and then Rook let out his breath.

"Okay," August said. "What the hell was that?"

"I'll explain. I'll explain everything. But first let's get Evan something to eat."

Chapter Eighteen

On the living room floor in front of the roaring fireplace, Rook lay on his back and Evan sat beside him. Rook had a pillow under his head. Evan had taken off his socks and stretched his legs out toward the heat of the fire, wiggling his toes.

The flickering light was bright on Evan's face, dancing in his brown eyes as he watched the flames. On the floor next to him was an almost empty bowl with the remains of shepherd's pie caked to the inside. Evan had eaten two big bowls and drunk three glasses of water. Rook had also eaten, which had been a surprise to both of them.

"But you said you never eat," Evan had said.

"Yet here I am eating."

The meal had made them both full and warm and tired. The smell of wood smoke was like a blanket in the air. But the desire to lay down his head had not yet come to Evan. He was excited, happy even. He sat with his legs drawn up and his chin on his knees and looked at Rook.

"Are you okay now?" Evan asked. "Does it still hurt?"

"It's getting better."

"That's good."

Rook said nothing more. He was staring up at the ceiling. It was white swirling stucco. He thought of August and he was thankful for her hospitality but embarrassed for his imposition. He could picture her upstairs lying in bed, just as she had as a child, tracing the intricacies of the ceiling with her eyes, filled with questions and wondering, unwilling to sleep. It was their familiarity with the night that allowed her and Rook such a close bond. Ever since she had been a child, whenever Rook arrived at the house in the silent hours, it was always August who found him, as if she had been waiting.

Rook wondered how different the young woman's life would have been if she had never met him, if he had left her whole family alone from the start. Certainly better, he thought, certainly easier. And what more was he bringing into her life now? *Who* had he brought into her home, already?

Rook drew a breath. "Evan," he said. "We can't stay here. We have to leave in the morning."

Still resting with his chin on his knuckles, Evan filled his cheeks with air and then blew them out with a pop.

Rook asked, "Do you understand? We have to keep going. We have to go to the church."

Evan lifted his head. "Why?"

"Because that's where you'll be safe." The words were like rotten food he had to spit out. *What a damn liar I am*, he thought.

"But I thought I was safe with *you*," Evan said. "You said nothing in this world can—"

"I can't protect you anymore."

"Why not?"

"Because I can't."

"But why?"

Rook sighed. "I just have to get you to the church and that's it. Then we're done. Then all of this is done."

Evan became very still. He uncrossed his legs and hugged his knees. The fire crackled. After a while he asked, "What if I don't want to go?"

"You have no choice."

"Yes I do."

Rook sat up, wincing a little in pain, but his face was severe. "You're going to the church, boy."

"No. I don't want to. I'm not going."

"You've known this all along. Why are you fighting me now?"

"'Cause I don't want to leave you!"

Something heavy caught in Rook's throat. He stared at Evan and breathed through his nose. Evan looked into the fire, his chin resting on his kneecaps. His eyes were rounded in the light.

When he spoke, his voice was small but serious. "I used to have a dream about you," he said. "Before all of this. Before I even met you. I had a dream that you came and found me. It was a scary dream at first and I never liked it. But then I *did* like it. And I'd wait for it. Like I knew it would come true."

Rook studied the fire. He didn't want to hear this. He knew it would only make things harder. But he was speaking before he realized it. "What was the dream about?" he asked.

Evan went on. "I'm running. It's really dark and really cold, and there's lots of streets, and I'm looking for something, but I don't know what it is. I just know I have to find it. Like it's something I lost and I have to get it back.

"And all around me the dark parts of the streets keep changing and moving like they're made of mud and worms and when I look over my shoulders behind me I see all the shadows coming after me, growing arms and legs in the shapes of people.

"They're all different. Some are these big monkeys and some look more like spiders, and they aren't wearing any clothes, and they're all hairy, and some of them are covered in poo, too, and they're always touching each other and chasing me."

Rook shifted onto his other elbow and listened.

Evan said, "And my heart's going so fast in the dream. I can hear it. Booming in my head. And so I just run and run. I try to hide but they always find me. And nothing can stop them. These scary people, like hungry monsters. It always feels like they want to eat me or if they catch me they'll rip me up. So I just run. And then finally I always come to a wall. A giant cement wall and there's no windows in it and no more streets. Nowhere left to run. That's the scariest part in the dream because I'm alone and I'm trapped. I always hate getting to that part.

"But sometimes I make myself go that far. I try to hold on and stay asleep because that's the part when you show up. I look up and I see this big, bright light. And all the shadows shrink away from it. And when I look in the light I see there's someone inside it. A man. And he's all made of fire. And then he comes down and picks me up in his arms and lifts me high above all the streets and we just stay there and look down and see the whole world stretching forever in the darkness."

Evan had been looking at his feet this whole time and at that moment he raised his head and looked Rook in the face. "You're the man made of fire," he said. "And you really came and took me away. And I didn't see it at first, but now I do. Now I see it. I want to stay with you."

For a while Rook said nothing. He was looking into the fire, now burned low, and whatever he saw seemed far away. Absently, he placed another log onto the bright coals. Soon it was crackling and ablaze. Rook lay down again with his head again on the pillow. Neither of them spoke, but between them the fire crackled and burned.

Evan slid across the floor until he was beside Rook and then he turned and lay down on his side and nuzzled against Rook's left arm. When Rook felt Evan against him, he lifted his arm and held Evan close to his own warmth. Evan closed his eyes.

"Rook?" he whispered.

"Yes."

"I'll go to the church with you, if you want me to."

"How come?"

"Because if we go together then that's okay. Then afterwards, when it's all over, I can come and live with you."

That same weight came again into Rook's throat, only this time he was without the help of gravity to push it down. He shut his eyes tight.

Evan asked, "Do you promise I can come back and live with you?"

The fire crackled.

"Rook, do you promise?"

"I promise," the man said.

Evan nestled even closer to Rook.

He whispered, "And maybe we can go down that river. Maybe we can get all the way to the ocean like you said? Could we do that, Rook?"

"Okay, Evan. Okay."

Evan smiled as he welcomed sleep like one who has finally, at last, found a bed that's his own.

After a while, Rook felt a change in Evan's breathing on his arm and he knew him to be fully asleep. He lay very still and held him. He stared at the spiralled stucco ceiling above. At the swirling patterns of its creation. In his peripheral vision, Rook's shadow and the shadow of the boy in his arms flickered in the firelight across the wall. Rook considered this dark mirroring. He looked at it a long time. As the fire burned down, he watched that phantom vision fade and be subsumed into the real and ever encroaching darkness of the room and he knew then what he had to do.

"Okay," he whispered. "Okay."

Rook lifted his arm from around Evan and sat up and then

carefully gathered Evan from the floor and stood. The pain in his abdomen was a dull ache.

He carried Evan upstairs to the spare room that August had prepared and laid him down in the bed, covering him with the duvet up to his chin. Evan slept soundly and Rook went out and down the hall towards the room with the light on.

CHAPTER NINETEEN

In the hallway, he could smell cigarette smoke. It was dry and faintly sweet and it calmed him as he approached. He knocked at August's door.

"Come in."

Rook pushed the door open and saw August sitting up in her bed. Her hair was down and it hung over her shoulders. She was waiting for him, like always. She had the ashtray on her lap over the blankets and a book laid open beside her. She tapped her cigarette once and smoked and watched Rook as he crossed to the foot of her bed.

"How's the kid?" she asked.

"Asleep."

August smoked. "So, what's up?"

"I wanted to say thank you, and again, my apologies for the intrusion."

"Rook, this is your house more than mine."

Rook steadied his eyes on the foot of the bed. "Anyway, we'll be leaving tomorrow."

"You can stay as long as you need, obviously."

"No. We should be going." Rook paused, and then, "So I should say goodbye."

"Why do I get the feeling you mean goodbye *forever*?"

Rook said nothing.

"Does this have to do with the boy?"

"Everything has to do with the boy now."

"Right." August put out her cigarette with a hiss. "Rook, are you going to actually tell me what's going on?"

Rook walked to the end of the room and laid his hands on the edge of the dresser and hung his head. August watched him. She could see the muscles of his back through his shirt and she saw him draw a deep breath and then let it out with a shudder. She had known Rook her whole life and yet in that moment he seemed like a total stranger.

"Rook?" she said, almost nervous.

"I've never told you," Rook started. "But you remind me a lot of the woman who first lived in this house. You always have."

"You mean Allison?"

"Yes. She would have liked you. You have the same way of thinking about things. Not getting worked up, but allowing the possibility, accepting the possibility of something. You were like that right from the start. I remember. You always accepted that I was . . ."

"Well it wasn't like I really had a choice, Rook. I mean it wasn't like some silly family legend. You were standing right in front of me, year after year. Never aging. Never changing. I'd say I *had* to accept it."

"No, everyone *had* to accept it, but you were the only one who truly did. You were the only one who was willing to believe it. I'm sorry, I'm trying to say thank you."

"Well, you're welcome," she said.

Rook swept his hair back and rubbed his face with both hands. Then he turned around. "What do I do?" he asked.

August laughed. "My god, Rook. I don't even know what your problem is." She reached for her cigarette case and lighter.

"The boy. That's my problem. I thought this was simple. I find the kid, take him to the church, and I get to be with Allison. But if I take him to the church, they're going to kill him."

"Who's going to kill him?"

"The one I met calls himself Gabriel, but he speaks of others. I don't know what they are, but they aren't human."

August was half-smiling as she lit the new cigarette and Rook recognized the look as one he'd seen on her face countless times, a little girl enthralled with shadows and spirits.

"Why would they want to kill the boy?" she asked.

"Evan isn't a normal boy. He's like me, but he's more. I can hear his heartbeat in my head like it's calling out to me, and it sounds like there are two hearts beating together. I think somehow Evan is the one that made me like this. The one that came to me the night Allison was killed. It said one day it would call to me, needing my help. And tonight I heard its voice again, out in the field. The same voice I heard years ago. The voice was coming from Evan. Somehow it's bound to him."

"So what, you think he's some kind of god?"

"No," Rook said. "I think he's the Devil. Gabriel said they would meet their Adversary. I think they plan to kill him."

August tapped her ash and nodded gravely. "Wow," she said. "So that would make this Gabriel guy, what, an angel or something?"

"I don't know."

"Rook if you actually believe this, maybe you should take him to the church. Let these people deal with him. What if he's dangerous?"

"That boy asleep in the other room is not evil. Am I supposed to take him to his death because one day he might turn out to be? In that case, drown every child the moment it's born. I can't do that. I will not."

August smoked. "Well, it sounds like you've made up your mind," she said. "But I don't see why you have to say goodbye."

Rook nodded and said, "There is one other thing."

Chapter Twenty

The sound of voices woke him. They were hushed but still he heard the back and forth of conversation. Evan opened his eyes. It was dark and the bed was soft, fresh, and clean smelling and the duvet was warm around him. He rolled over and his face was wet on the pillow; he wiped the drool from his cheek with the back of his hand. He heard the voices again. At first, he just listened, as the sounds were far away and came mixed with his dreams, but the more he heard Rook's voice the more he stirred.

The door to his room was open and there was faint light in the hall. Half asleep, he slid from the bed and tiptoed across the floor. The hardwood was cold on his bare feet.

He reached the door and stopped in the threshold against the frame and peered out. He could see down the hall to the top of the staircase. The light hit the curve of the wooden banister. At the end of the hall was the open door from which Rook's voice sounded.

Evan tiptoed out to the top of the stairs and crouched by the banister, holding onto the balusters, his face pressed between them. He listened.

He could hear very little. Rook's gruff voice did not carry well and August's was a near whisper.

"... Oath breaker ... just a matter of time."

"... Rook ... give them the boy ..."

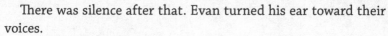

There was silence after that. Evan turned his ear toward their voices.

"... Where will you ... ?"

"... As far as we can ..."

The rest fell below his hearing. He shuffled forward, keeping hold of the balusters. He sat and listened again for Rook's voice.

"... August ... your whole damn life ... I'm sorry."

"I've never thought ... apologetic type ... please, don't say anymore."

Once more there was silence. Evan's knees were stiff and his feet were itchy and he shifted his weight against the banister. Then he heard the floor squeak and it sounded as if Rook were coming out into the hall.

Evan dashed back to his room and jumped into the bed. He pulled the duvet up to his chin and closed his eyes. He lay very still.

After a few minutes, he heard the door creak and felt Rook's presence in the room. He lay very still and pretended to be asleep. He listened for the sound of Rook's feet on the hardwood but they were silent. He thought he could hear Rook's slow, tired breathing. It could have been the noise of the wind from outside. Finally, the door closed, hushing the room into darkness.

CHAPTER TWENTY-ONE

Evan slept late. When he woke, the midmorning light had flooded the room and he heard the chirping of house sparrows. A crow cawed and it sounded like it was right outside the window. Evan sat up. The sky was bright blue.

He stretched his arms above his head. His mouth was dry and he was thirsty. Across the room on a cushioned footstool, he saw his pants and socks and a sweater had been washed and laid folded there for him. All at once he wanted to get up and go find Rook. He was excited at the thought. He dressed and went downstairs. The house was bright and clean, the hardwood floor a rich amber, golden in the light.

A hope came to Evan that maybe he would get to stay here and live with Rook.

In the kitchen, August was drying her hands. When she turned and saw Evan, she gasped, clasping her hands to her breast.

"Gosh, you startled me," she said, and then laughed.

"I'm sorry," Evan said. "Can I have a glass of water?"

"Sure."

"Where's Rook?" Evan asked.

"I'm not sure. But he'll come back."

Evan went into the dining room and sat at the table. The room smelled of cigarette smoke and the deeper, richer scent of the fireplace. Rook's pillow still lay on the floor. Evan wondered when Rook would be back.

There was a smaller room off from the dining room, and where Evan sat at the table he could see in through the open door. The walls were lined with high bookcases, and there was a big wooden desk in the middle of the room.

August came into the dining room with a glass of water and placed it on the table. Evan sat forward. The high wooden back of the dining-table chair arched above his head and he looked very small. August sat down across from him.

"You just want the water?" she asked. "You don't want milk or juice or something?"

Evan shook his head and sipped the water. "Are those all your books?" he asked.

August glanced to the open doorway of her office. "Yep, every one."

"Why do you have so many?"

"Well, I read a lot, for starters. And others I use for work."

"Are you a librarian?"

"No," she said and half laughed. "I'm a writer."

"Oh. What do you write about?"

"Well . . ." August drew the word out and sounded oddly reluctant. "I write about strange things. I write stories about the *unknown*, glimpses, encounters, mysteries."

"You mean about ghosts and stuff?"

"Sometimes. The hidden world is much more than just ghosts. And since it's all *mostly* made-up stories, I can do whatever I want."

Evan nodded, though he didn't really understand what August had said. He sipped his glass of water. August opened her slim gold-rimmed case and slid out a cigarette and lit it with a match. The smoke trailed in the light of the window.

"Do you like books?" August asked.

Evan shrugged. "Not really."

"How old are you?"

"Six. But I'm almost seven."

August gave him a quizzical look. "You don't seem like an almost-seven-year-old," she said.

"I know. I'm different."

"No, you just seem more grown up." August quickly added, "What do you want to be when you *do* grow up?"

Evan was surprised at the question. He had never really thought about that. His brow crinkled. "I want to . . . make things *right*. I want one of those hammers that you bang on the high table."

"You mean you want to be a judge?"

Evan nodded and sipped his water, keeping the glass tipped at his mouth.

They were quiet. August watched Evan. He could feel her eyes like static heat on his skin, and it reminded him of being at the Centre, how people would look at him He glanced once at her and then he looked at the table. August tapped her cigarette into the ashtray.

Eventually, Evan asked, "So, are you Rook's wife?"

August laughed outright. She took a drag of her cigarette and two grey jets shots out her nose. "No," she said. "I'm certainly not his wife."

"Oh. So how do you know him?"

August looked at Evan as if measuring his aptitude to understand what she was about to say. After a moment, she said, "I first met Rook when I was four years old, and for many years I thought he was our neighbour or a friend of my parents. He came and went. Then when I was eleven I saw my first ghost, a *real* ghost. After that, I looked at everything differently. I saw Rook for what he was."

"What is he?"

"You don't know?" She sounded surprised.

Evan shook his head. He knew Rook was different, like him, but that was all.

"Well, Rook's more like a living ghost. He was born in the 1760s and he's been alive ever since. He built this house, lived in it with his wife and son. After what happened, Rook became bound to the house. It was smaller back then, just this room and the kitchen. Different owners over the years must have built on the rest. My parents bought this house when I was one or two, and Rook was here then. I used to call him Uncle Rook, but he's not my uncle. He's just my oldest friend. When my parents decided to sell the house, I bought it, and Rook was here. I'm not ashamed to say that I've made most of my money from the books I've written about Rook."

August put out her cigarette and got up and went into the kitchen. Evan heard cupboard doors open, the fridge, the clink of ceramics, and then the sloshing sound of rinsing water.

August returned to the table with a mug of coffee and a glass of milk and set the latter in front of Evan.

"You can't just want water," she said.

Evan thanked her and sipped the milk.

August sat down and held her coffee mug with both hands.

"So . . . Rook's like one hundred years old?" Evan asked.

"He's more like two hundred and fifty years old, almost."

"Wow," Evan said. He looked at August. "How old are you?" he asked.

August narrowed her eyes. "How old do you think I am?"

"Umm . . . thirty?"

A smile flashed across her face. "That's sweet," she said. "I'm forty-three."

"Oh."

For the first time, Evan looked straight into the woman's eyes. They were green and almost yellowish and he saw the wrinkles at their edges. He blinked and looked away again to admire the many books. August sipped her coffee and lit another cigarette, extinguishing the match with a wave in the air.

After a while, Evan asked, "So what does Rook do with you?"

"*Do* with me?" August said, puzzled, sounding a little affronted even. "He doesn't *do* anything with me. Like I said, he comes and goes. In my late twenties, we spent a lot of time together. I managed to convince him in a weak moment to let me interview him. Extensively. That's when I got most of the material for the books. But I don't actually see him very often at all anymore."

Evan's brow furrowed. He tilted his head. He was about to ask another question, but it was then that Evan heard August's voice— he *felt* it.

I don't want him to leave. . . .

It was a swift infiltrating whisper that reached across the table and split through his chest.

Evan looked up and saw August's green eyes shimmering. He said nothing. He could see the sadness in her face plain as if she had told him she was about to cry.

Her voice came to him again.

He's scared and he's running. He says he has no choice, but that's a lie. He's lying to himself. Choice is all he has. He's been on his own for so long, always done what he wants. But now he's not thinking about himself. He's made the choice to let himself go. I don't want him to leave.

Evan was listening with rapt attention, her voice like an ephemeral hum inside his head, a weight in the centre of him. He almost didn't notice when August started to speak aloud again.

She had lit a new cigarette and was saying, "You know, the truth about Rook is that he does all of this because he believes he owes it to someone. Because of what happened in his past, he feels he has to atone for it. But he's such an old fool. And I mean that literally, he's *old*. He's stuck in an old-world mentality, where men believe in bullshit like honour—pardon my French—and all it ever does is get them killed."

Evan was a little confused and overwhelmed with everything August was telling him, but nevertheless he wanted to hear more.

August shook her head. "Really, I can't explain Rook," she said. "He's been the proof in my life that there is more to this world than anyone knows. And I believe it. But most days it's just easier to pretend that he isn't real, that I'm crazy, or he's just a figment of my imagination. Just a dream. Then, of course, he shows up like this."

Evan watched as tears ran down August's cheeks. She wiped them away as quickly as they fell, looking almost surprised.

"I have to ask," August said. "Do you know why Rook came and found you? Do you know what this is all about?"

Evan put his elbows on the table and rested his chin on his hands. "Sometimes I feel like I don't belong . . . in this world. But maybe I belong wherever Rook is, wherever he goes. 'Cause when I'm with Rook I don't feel like that anymore. I feel like I have a home."

August's expression lightened and she smiled. When she spoke, her voice was smooth. "I think you're right," she said. "You take care of him. Okay?"

"I will," Evan said.

●

August and Evan ate a small breakfast of scrambled eggs and toast, and then August said she had work to do and went into her office. She closed the door. Rook still hadn't returned.

Evan lay on the couch in the living room where he could hear the clicking of computer keys from inside August's office. At one point the clicking stopped and Evan was certain he heard the sound of

Rook's voice. He listened, but there was silence. Then the clicking resumed. After a while, Evan fell asleep.

When he woke, there was a blanket over him and he was drooling. He wiped his mouth and sat up. The house was quiet. The door to August's office was open and there was a note on the coffee table beside him.

Have gone for groceries. Stay in the house. – August.

Evan kicked away the blanket and slid off the couch.

"Rook?" he called.

There was no answer. He wandered out to the front hall and called Rook's name again. After a moment, he went into August's office. Again, he called Rook's name, though it was clear that he wasn't there.

In addition to the books on the walls, there were many stacked on August's desk as well. Evan went around it and climbed into her chair. The springs creaked a little. There was a small squished pillow at the low back of the chair and Evan sat forward away from it.

On the desk, August's laptop was open. There were sheets of paper all over the place, covered in tiny handwriting, and a sky-blue coffee mug crammed full of pens and pencils.

Evan swivelled in the chair, swinging his legs, then grabbed the edge of the desk to stop himself. His fingers knocked August's computer mouse and her laptop screen brightened. There was a picture on the screen.

At first, Evan failed to grasp what he was seeing. There was a man in a grey suit sitting in an armchair, rather slumped, his face downturned. His hair was dark and combed back. His large hands held the ends of the chair arms like widespread spider legs. He was not an old man, Evan decided, but he gave the impression of age. He looked tired.

The screen dimmed and Evan touched the mouse again to awaken it. When the mouse pointer moved across the screen, little play and pause buttons appeared over the image and Evan realized it was a video. His hand went clammy on the mouse.

This is a video of Rook.

The thought made his heart jump. Evan glanced over the top of the laptop to the office door, nervous, waiting to see if in the next second or two someone would arrive and catch him. Could he really do this? Could he watch the video of Rook? He waited another second. Then he pressed *play*.

The video started. At first Rook sat slumped and still in the armchair. He stared at the floor. Evan watched him with rapt attention.

Then there was a voice. "Can you tell me about what happened next?"

It was August's voice. Evan realized that she must have been sitting behind the video camera.

Rook shifted, holding his gaze to a spot on the floor. He huffed once and Evan smiled. Then Rook said, "You mean, you want to know how I became what I am now. You want to know how I became one with darkness?"

August's voice was a hard stone when she said, "Yes, tell me."

A moment's silence. Then Rook said, "I had work in town under a young carpenter named Absalom Shade, building a new church steeple."

"The man who you worked for, building the mill?"

"We built the whole town."

"And what about your wife?"

"Allison, she had a good hand as a seamstress. She could fashion anything, but her dresses were the best. They made your head spin— that someone could put such beautiful detail into a thing."

"And then?"

"Would you like to hear this, or would you rather piece it together yourself?"

It sounded like August laughed. "I'm sorry. Go ahead."

Rook went on. "With the post office built and the store opening, Shade's Mills was growing and people were moving there. It was turning into a really nice town. The landowner, Mr. William Dickson, had an event to celebrate it, inviting people from all over, but mostly from Hamilton and Waterloo. He hired a circus troupe from god knows where, and I remember when they came down the road in their wagons, you could hear the carts rattling and jingling from miles away. They had donkeys braying and a roaring lion in a cage. A fortnight later, half of Shade's Mills was sick with fever, myself included. I was bedridden."

"I'm sorry? You got sick?" August asked.

Rook nodded. "They had to send for the doctor in Waterloo. It was cholera. And it damned near killed half the town."

Rook paused and shook his head.

Then he said, "We'd had our first child two months before. A boy, Nathaniel, named after Allison's father. It was midwinter and there I was, like a dying dog, unable to get out of bed. I couldn't even hold my son. There'd been talk of men camping around the town and on the roads. Sick and hungry and cold. Unable to go on with the circus they had come through with. I don't know if the men who came to our house that night were from the troupe. It doesn't matter. They were drifters in any case."

"They came to your home?"

Again, Rook nodded. "Allison had Nathaniel sleeping, bundled up tight on the cot near the stove, away from me to keep from catching my sickness. I was in the bed. I remember there was a knock at the door. But I don't remember if Allison opened the door or if they kicked it in—I was mad with fever. I remember the noise of pots and pans rattling, drawers being pulled out and crashing to the floor as they looked for food. Then I remember trying to stand up and one of them cracked me in the face with a rifle butt. I remember lying on the floor, trying to breathe. Allison was yelling and screaming. I saw her rush across the room and cover the cot with her body. One of the men shot her in the back. They took all they could carry and were gone. I forced myself up and went to Allison where she had fallen over the cot, over Nathan. The bullet had gone straight through her breast. Gone through them both. My wife and son were dead."

"What did you do after that?" August said.

"You mean, how did I become like this? I suppose that's what you've been waiting for."

"If you think you can go on, I'd like to know."

Rook started to speak, but August cut him off.

"Oh shit," she said. "Hang on, the battery's about to crap out."

With a sudden cut to black, the video ended.

Evan sat for a moment, then slipped off the chair and walked out into the living room. The house seemed darker, as if it had come under a cloud. It made him want to scream or shout to clear his feelings away. But there was no one to hear him. He found his boots and his peacoat in the hall closet, dressed, and left the house.

Outside, it was warmer than he had expected. The air was dry and it smelled clean and fresh. His head cleared a little. The sun shone on the snow, bright and glittering, and Evan felt better. He wandered aimlessly and found himself in the back yard.

His feet sunk deep holes through the snow and he had to lift his legs high to walk. It made him feel like Rook. He gestured behind him as he trudged along and said, "Come on. Pick up your feet. Let's go."

He shuffled down the hill to the bottom of the yard where an old wire fence was strung, beyond which were pine trees. The fence was rusted and sagging and there were the dormant remains of wild creeper vine entwined through it. A heavy silence clung to the area. It was colder at the bottom of the yard, in the shadow of the house, and Evan shivered.

At that moment, the cloudy feeling in Evan's head cleared away, and he realized that he was alone, not merely in the yard but truly in his whole life. He had never imagined such a thing before and it made him feel panicky. He tried to argue with himself that he wasn't alone. He had Rook. But Rook was also alone, and that's what Evan now realized with even greater clarity. Rook had lost his family. He was alone and all by himself and that was why he wasn't afraid of anything. Rook was strong because he was alone. These thoughts came and went all at once, but they left Evan with an indescribable feeling of himself and the world. As much as he was frightened, he was also filled with a new calm, as if someone had let him in on a great secret. He felt *right* being alone.

He walked along the fence to the end of the yard and then he turned and looked up.

Rook stood at the top of the hill.

It was the first time Evan had seen Rook since the night before and he did not smile, but he felt his face flush and his stomach tingled with nervous excitement. The new feeling he'd had about himself and his place in the world went away in a flash. All Evan wanted was Rook.

Rook came down the hill, his feet making deep lines in the snow. He wore a fresh grey button-down shirt under his heavy coat and a pair of clean black pants. His beard was trimmed and his hair combed back. In the sunlight it seemed to Evan as if for the first time he was seeing Rook's true face. He looked like an ordinary man, prepared for some service or ceremony.

"What are you doing?" Rook said.

"I wanted to go outside," Evan said, and then, "Where did you go?"

"For a walk."

"You were gone a long time"

"It was a long walk."

Rook looked past Evan to the thicket beyond the fence as if he had seen something move. Evan followed Rook's gaze. A shifting, creeping sense came over them both that they were being watched.

"Come on," Rook said. "It's time to go."

— —

When they came inside, August was in the kitchen chopping carrots and potatoes on a wooden cutting board. She heard the front door open and came out into the foyer. She knew they were leaving, even before Rook said anything.

"So you've made up your mind, then?" August asked.

"I have. Though it's not much of a choice."

"Yes it is. Don't think it isn't."

Rook said nothing.

"Are you leaving right now?"

"We're going to take the truck. It's not safe if we stay here."

"Well, you better get going, then." She looked at Evan. "Remember what I said, you take care of him."

Evan nodded.

"Thank you," Rook said. "For everything."

August closed her eyes and gave a small laugh. "You stupid old fool," she said.

"Goodbye, August."

"Goodbye, Rook."

Chapter Twenty-Two

Rook and Evan drove out of Shade's Mills in a red Ford pickup truck. Neither of them spoke. The road was a two-lane country highway marked on one side by a snow-filled marsh of frozen cattails and on the other side by wooded hills. There wasn't a soul in sight.

The afternoon sky was clear and blue and for this Rook was pleased. He checked the rear-view mirror often. They had the heaters going and it was warm with the sunlight across their laps. The cab smelled of cigarettes and little else.

After a while, Evan broke their silence. "Is the church very far?" he asked.

"It's just through those trees," Rook said with a nod to the right side of the road.

Evan looked out his window at the woods. The trees were thin and grey and there were many dead ones fallen over the ground. But he saw no sign of a church.

"I don't see it," he said.

"It's there. Though it's just a bunch of old stones. The ruins of a church."

"Then why are we going there?"

"We're not," Rook said.

Evan looked back. "Why not?"

"I lied to you," Rook said. "I said you'd be safe at the church but that's not true."

"You *lied*?" Evan said.

Rook said nothing. He watched the road. After a moment, he glanced down and saw Evan crying. It robbed him of breath. The pain in his abdomen spiked for a moment. He checked the rearview mirror and then pulled the truck off onto the shoulder of the road and parked. He shut off the ignition and faced Evan.

"Now listen to me," he said. "Stop crying. I did a lot of thinking this morning and I've decided that I can't take you to the church. There are *mean* people there. Do you understand?"

"Why did you lie to me?"

Rook shook his head. "Because there was something that I wanted before. I swore an oath to find you and bring you to the church, and in return I would get to see my wife and son again. But I can't do that anymore."

Evan remembered the video of Rook talking about his family. *The bullet had gone straight through her breast. Gone through them both. My wife and son were dead.*

He blinked and wiped his cheeks, sniffing back his tears. Then he bowed his head. When he spoke his voice was small but firm.

"You can take me to the church, Rook. It's okay. Then you can be with your family again."

Rook grabbed Evan and pulled him close and held him. Evan hugged him back and felt his whole body tucked against the warmth and weight of Rook's chest.

Right here is where I want to be, Evan thought.

Rook let Evan go and sat back.

"Rook?" Evan said.

"Yes?"

"What are we? I mean, how did you become . . ." Evan paused to recall the words, then said, ". . . *one with the darkness*?"

"I asked for it," Rook said. "A long time ago, the night my family was taken from me, I prayed for it."

"You prayed? You mean to God?"

"At first I called to God, and then I pleaded to anything that would hear me. Finally, something answered."

"What was it?"

"It was just a voice. A calm, plainly spoken voice. Cold at first, then warm like a fire. It said, *'It's okay. I have you. Let me help.'* And I welcomed it."

"What did you do?" Evan said.

"I went out into the night and I found the men who had killed Allison and my boy. I tracked them through the snow down along the river to where they'd camped. It was dark but they'd built a fire and I could see its light from where I was. That was when the night came. It gave me strength like nothing in this world, and I tore those men apart with my bare hands. I welcomed something evil into my heart that night, and ever since I've been a man and a monster."

"Am I evil?" Evan said.

"No, Evan. You are *strong*. You are good and kind and brave, and that's all you need to be."

Evan's eyes welled as he said, "You're going to leave me, aren't you? That's why you're saying all of this. Because you have to go away."

"Yes," Rook said. "I'm breaking my oath. I don't know when, but eventually they will come for me."

"I won't let them hurt you," Evan stated.

A smile touched Rook's eyes as he looked at Evan. "We'll go as far as we can," he said.

"What do I do when you're gone?"

"I don't know, Evan, but I think *you* do. Or you will."

Evan's brow creased, uncertain whether he should agree or disagree. Before he could say anything, Rook went on.

"I was told that this would happen," Rook said.

"You were?"

"The voice that answered my prayers that night told me that one day it would call on me for help. Over the years, it came to speak with me often. At first it was a torment. I felt cursed. I could see a face sometimes when it spoke to me. Eyes like fire. And I hated it. I hated what it had done to me, and I blamed it for everything. But over the years, the voice became a comfort, a friend even. It asked endless questions, curious to know about us, about people, about life. And it told me stories, too. Everything you think I know about God and the Devil I learned from this voice."

Evan remembered their conversation in the cave around the fire. The things Rook had claimed were just ideas now felt real in Evan's recollection. He remembered them now almost as if they had been his own ideas instead of Rook's.

Rook went on. "The last time I heard that voice was almost seven years ago. Until the other night in the cornfield when I heard that same voice coming from you. I believe this has been its call for help."

"This?"

"Yes, Evan. About a year ago I started hearing this sound in my head, a steady throbbing. Sometimes it was calm, other times it pounded like a drum. It was a heartbeat. It was your heartbeat, Evan, calling out to me. It's the reason I started looking for you, and it's how I've been able to find you. Do you understand? You are different, Evan. You can hear people's thoughts. You can make them do what you want. You can call the night. Don't you know who you are?"

Evan was silent, a receptive yet pensive look on his face. He seemed on the verge of speaking, when Rook turned away all of a sudden. A harsh voice had cut across the stillness of the afternoon, and Rook's stomached dropped.

Oath breaker . . .

"What is it?" Evan asked, having heard nothing.

Rook ignored Evan. He looked out across the frozen marsh. The snow was glaringly bright in the sun and he squinted as he tried to scan the horizon. He glanced in the rear-view mirror, then turned around and looked out the back of the truck's cab.

There was someone walking up the road behind them. A slim figure, going along in a lazy way.

It wasn't Gabriel. Rook knew that and was relieved. More than anything else, it looked like a drifter, Rook thought. Just a hitchhiker, walking alone.

Evan pulled on Rook's sleeve. "Rook," he said. "Rook, there's someone out in front of the truck."

Gabriel stood out in front of the truck, his feet on either side of the yellow median. He was staring straight at Rook and Evan. His silver hair looked like liquid metal in the sun, and he was dressed neatly in a beige overcoat with three black buttons fastened down the front. His collar was folded down, but the angle of the sun made a shadow of his face.

Rook's right hand clicked the lock mechanism of Evan's seatbelt and the belt went limp over Evan's lap, then zipped up into the corner.

"Run, Evan," Rook said. "Get out of the truck and run to the woods."

"But what about—"

"I'll be right behind you. Now, go!"

Evan opened the truck's door and hopped down. He looked back at Rook and their eyes met. In that moment, Evan felt Rook's voice flow through him like a cool wind.

I wish I could stay with you. . . .

"Rook?" Evan said aloud, his eyes welling up.

"I said *run*, Evan!"

Evan turned and took off like a shot towards the woods. There was a ditch of deep snow off the shoulder of the road and he slipped and slid down into it, gathered himself quick, and scrambled up the other side.

Evan ran and didn't look back, arms pumping, and knees kicking up. Then he was in the woods, the tall, barren pine trees encircling him.

Chapter Twenty-Three

Rook stepped out of the truck. The sun was bright on his face. A crow cawed from somewhere in the marshes and from far away the rushing of the river carried. Rook closed the door and turned, but not before catching sight of the hitchhiker still walking slowly up the road from behind them. He paused.

Closer now, yet still indistinct against the glare of the sun, Rook could see that the stranger walked with an uneven gait. A lame leg, he imagined. But then a deeper realization came to him, and he knew it was no hitchhiker at all. His first thought was that it was one of Gabriel's partners. Gabriel often spoke of others, the many, *we*. Though Rook's gut told him he was wrong. He squinted to see better, and pictured the red-haired boy dragged beneath the van, presumably killed. *It couldn't be the boy*, Rook thought. But the *thing* within him could have possessed someone else.

Whoever or whatever it was, Rook didn't have the time to stand and wonder. He could hear Gabriel's fine footsteps clicking along the road, and he walked out around the front of the truck to meet him.

They both stopped a few feet from each other, Gabriel's hands clasped behind his back, Rook's at his sides.

"I won't bring Evan to his death," Rook said. "I've told—"

Gabriel wagged his forefinger in the air and *tsked*. "Save your breath, Rook. What's done is done. You made your choice."

"The boy is innocent, Gabriel."

"No one is innocent. Innocence is a mortal's idea, like one of their stories. It's the dream of life before it comes into being. After that, every creature on this earth is guilty of taking its first breath."

"So you're just going to kill him."

"The boy will play his part, as you did. Your change of heart came too late, I'm afraid. It will be easy to lure the boy to the church from here. I've come now only to deliver your penance. You did not think you could break your oath and simply walk away, did you? You must pay for your transgression."

"And how do suppose you're going to make me do that?"

"I'm not going to do anything," Gabriel said. "Your penance is placed in your own hands."

Rook's expression shifted with a glimmer of hope. *Maybe there's a way out of this*, he thought.

Gabriel went on: "You and the boy stayed well hidden from your pursuers, but there has been one searching for you most of all. You escaped it twice, but it has not stopped. It has, however, struggled to follow your signs. I didn't think that was fair, so I gave the ancient one a small amount of guidance."

Rook's heart sank. Somehow he knew what Gabriel would say next. And then it came.

"I sent the ancient one to your home," Gabriel said. "It met your dear August. She truly is a kind-hearted young woman. She tried to be nice. She even asked the demon its name."

"What the hell have you done?" Rook said.

"*I* have done very little at all."

Rook advanced on him and yelled, "*I* broke the oath! August had nothing to do with this!"

Gabriel raised his hands. "Before you tear my head off—much good it will do you—why don't you turn around and see for yourself what has happened?"

Rook paused and shuddered. Again, he knew what he would find if he turned around.

Not August, please.

In quick, painful flashes, Rook saw August standing in her kitchen washing dishes, the sink half-full with warm soapy water. She looked over her shoulder when the creature appeared. Nothing any ordinary person would have seen. A distortion in the air, perhaps. A transparent shroud hanging six feet above the floor. He saw August reach, as she had all her life, with an open hand towards the unknown. Then he saw her turn and run. He saw her screaming. And her face. Her eyes burned into shallow, blackened cavities like all those on the bus. Then she was walking down the middle of the road, driven forward, even on a broken leg, alone but for the thing that drove her.

For a moment Rook thought if he only stood still, looking straight ahead, he could make this go away. If he refused to turn around, he could refuse to let it be real.

But he could feel her—no, *it*—standing behind him. Like flaring static on the back of his neck. He forced himself to turn around.

He noticed August's left leg first—twisted at the hip, her jeans torn, her kneecap hooked inward—and then he looked up and saw her wholly. He looked her in the face. It was real. The pain tore through him like a knife in the chest and his fists clenched.

"What have they done to you?" he asked through gritted teeth.

August said nothing. Her arm rose from her side, and Rook knew that it was reaching for his throat. He lifted his chin willingly. *Why not let her?* Better to let this nightmare end by her hand than any other.

But it was not *her* hand that reached for him. It was this *thing*. Like the darkness that lived in Rook, only wilder. It must have possessed someone long ago and lost itself, warped by time into a roaming, suffering madness. Its presence felt like a nest of enraged hornets. And this creature had hold of August. It crouched on the seat of her soul. Rook couldn't bear it.

Rook looked again into August's face, searching for a sign of her real self. There had to be some remnant of her left. And then he saw it—somewhere underneath, deep within, buried behind the burned and blackened flesh of her eyes—he saw August's will still fighting. Some emotion moved over the ravaged face, as if a part of August was still trying to scream.

In that moment, whatever measure of hope Rook had found for himself over the last few days washed away and his body hummed in the stilled instance of its departure. He pictured Evan running and knew that the boy's life was out of his hands now. He was surprised to feel light and free.

All the days of his life seemed to disintegrate into mere moments of choice and action and nothing more. Taken as a whole his life was formless. He saw no sum creation, no man named Rook. For the first time in his life the concept of fate appealed to him. Its simplicity sparkled like sunlight in the snow. He had lacked the power to save his wife and son, but maybe he wasn't meant to save them. Maybe he had been given the strength of the night so that he might one day save August. And here it was, another moment in which to act, but no longer a choice at all.

Rook caught August's outstretched arm and pushed it to the side. His strength in conjuring the night was weakened in the daylight, but there was darkness within him and for this he would rally every ounce of it. He braced his free hand flat against her chest.

At the touch of his hand, the darkness that lived in Rook connected with the thing inside August. There was a moment of recognition, like two old comrades meeting in the street. They knew each other's names, both as ancient as any that had first stood upon the shores of Hell.

Rook shut his eyes, his palm beginning to heat, and he drew a deep breath. "Let her go," he whispered.

August wriggled and thrashed at Rook with her free hand, spitting and making low, guttural sounds, but Rook held her still. From under his hand on her chest, a bright light began to glow. And then Rook screamed out in pain, as he called the night from himself and commanded it one last time to drag the darkness from August.

He yelled, "Let her go!"

Rook's heart stopped—beat once—and blood spurted from his mouth. August's body recoiled from the touch of Rook's open palm, contorting grotesquely, her head whipping backwards as jets of black vapour shot out of her mouth and eyes. Like a great cloud of flies, the jets swarmed in the air above August, swirling and buzzing in an attempt to coalesce into a true form. What might have been wings beat the air as a long, hooked neck reeled back and a tormented howl cut across the country road. The seared and blackened flesh fell away from of August's eyes. Her body collapsed at the side of the road. The cloud of vapour dissipated.

Staggering, Rook dropped to his knees in front of the truck. He slumped back against the grill. But for the remnant heat of the engine warming his neck, Rook was growing cold all over. His head hung. He could feel the hard road under him and he thought either it was rising up or he was sinking into it. He lifted his head with great effort and looked across the road at August and waited for a sign. He mouthed her name, his voice wheezing. She lay still on her side, her face turned from him.

A shadow fell across Rook's shoulders. Gabriel stood over him. Rook coughed and his mouth filled with blood. He spat it out and looked up.

Gabriel was silhouetted against the sun. His darkened face seemed adorned with a ring of light and Rook found a crude hypocrisy in that. It made him want to laugh despite his mouthful of blood.

"You keep thinking you can save them," Gabriel said.

Rook was watching August again for signs of recovery.

Please . . .

"Did you really think it was possible for us to return Allison to life?"

Rook wasn't listening. August's right arm was draped behind her back, but he thought he saw her wrist twitch.

Please . . .

"Death knows no reunion," Gabriel said.

The words pierced Rook with an icy veracity. Fate was a fool's notion. August was not going to get up. She would *never* get up. It was all too late. He felt himself sinking, the cold earth drawing him down, and he thought of Evan out there alone. Running. What hope did the boy have? Rook's last thought was that he had failed all the people he loved.

Gabriel waited until Rook's eyes lost the ability to hold light and became flat and empty-looking. Then he started across the road to the woods.

Chapter Twenty-Four

Evan ran blindly. Wheezing and bleary-eyed and praying, if only to the trees that he ran past or to the cold wind that burned in his throat: *He'll be right behind me! He'll be right behind me!*

When at last he stopped, he collapsed panting to the ground and he lay on his back in the snow and the layered pine needles below. His chest quaked. He started to cry again.

"No," he snapped. "Stop that. He's coming. He's coming."

He lay still and waited, his chest heaving. Then he rolled over and looked up, scanning the woods. When he saw nothing and no one, he fell back into the snow. He closed his eyes and saw Rook telling him to run.

I wish I could stay with you. . . .

The tears came violently even as he tried to hold them back and he convulsed in the snow. He cried aloud.

"Stop it," he said to himself. "Stop crying."

Evan sat up again and looked back across the path of his flight through the woods. His feet were cold and he shivered.

"Come on, Rook. Come on."

He watched the low ridge where he had come up from the ditch and he waited. The forest was quiet.

Then he yelled, "Come on, Rook!"

Two chickadees flew out from the thicket and Evan jumped. He got down on his hands and knees and watched the tree line. A wind came up and swayed in the tops of the pines. Evan kept watching.

Nothing.

His peripheral vision darkened. He felt dizzy and his stomach turned over. He crawled forward a few feet, and then lowered his head and vomited. He wiped his mouth and then brushed the wetness from his eyes and cheeks.

The crunch of feet in the snow came from close by.

"Evan?"

Hearing his name, Evan jumped again. He looked up and saw a tall silver-haired man standing ten feet away beside a thin pine tree. It took a moment, but then he recognized his silver hair. It was the man from the hotel room where Rook had first taken him.

Evan scrambled away on the ground.

"It's okay, Evan. My name is Gabriel. I'm a friend. You're Evan, yes?"

Evan stopped but said nothing.

When Gabriel took a step forward, Evan flinched like a feral creature poised to run off, and Gabriel halted. He put up his hands and showed his palms. They looked soft and plump and delicate.

"You're Evan, aren't you?" Gabriel asked, his voice smooth and calm. Then, "I'm a friend of Rook's. He asked me to come out here to meet you. To help you. I helped you and Rook before, back in the city. Remember that?"

A look of stubborn, angry recollection flashed across Evan's face.

Gabriel said, "I visited you and Rook at the hotel, when Rook needed help getting out of the city. He needs help now to get you to a *church*."

"We aren't going to the church anymore," Evan said.

Gabriel raised his hands higher in the air as he took another foot forward. Evan shuffled back, but he was calm. He was watching the man's mouth. It opened wide when he spoke and each time revealed a host of white teeth. The sight was unnerving. But the sound of the man's voice was familiar. Evan remembered him talking to Rook in the hotel. He had come to help them, then, to warn them of the bad people. Hadn't he?

"You don't have to be scared," Gabriel said. "I'm not going to hurt you. I'm here to help. Rook asked me to help. He said something bad was going to happen to him. He said he knew he was going to—"

Evan cut him off. "Don't talk about Rook," he said.

"Evan, I'm just here to help. Rook asked me to come and look after you once he was gone. He told me everything. I know about the church. And I know about those people who want to hurt you. They're still coming, Evan. We have to get you safe."

"Rook said the church isn't safe. He said it was a lie."

Gabriel lowered his hands and nodded. "I'm so sorry," he said. "It's awful that you had to see Rook that way. He was very scared. And he was confused. He knew what was going to happen to him and he panicked."

Evan shook his head. "He wasn't scared."

"Yes he was. He knew he was going to die."

"Don't say that," Evan said and then began to cry.

"Rook is dead, Evan. I'm sorry, but you have to face that."

Evan yelled, "Don't talk about Rook!" He sprang to his feet and started running back the way he had come.

At the edge of the woods, he slipped down the slope into the ditch, picked himself up, and climbed back up to the road. He ran to the front of the truck and stopped.

Rook sat against the grill of the truck with his arms slack at his sides, his legs splayed out and his chin hung to his chest. His beard was clumped with blood. Evan stared.

Then he shouted, "Get up!"

Rook said nothing.

Evan stepped towards him and spoke clearly. "Get up, Rook. Let's go. We have to keep going. Come on." He kicked Rook's left boot and yelled. "Get up!"

A black bird flew up from the river and whirled in the air and swooped down across the road and rose back over the woods. Evan failed to see it. He was glaring hard at Rook and his eyes welled.

Evan crouched in front of Rook and pushed him with both hands, then hit Rook in the chest with his fists.

He yelled, "You promised! You promised I'd get to go with you. Why'd you promise if you were going to leave me?"

He grabbed the collar of Rook's jacket and tried to pull him up and Rook's head rolled and Evan saw his flat, glossy eyes and he jumped back.

Gabriel stood behind Evan in the sun. He said, "He's not coming back, Evan. You're all alone now."

"What happened to him?" Evan asked.

"The mean people killed him."

Evan started crying.

"But I'm here to help you," Gabriel said. "Rook's last hope was that I would get you to the church, so you would be safe. The mean people are still coming for you."

Evan wiped his face clear with both hands. His eyes were puffy and red. He stared at Rook. Then he stood.

Gabriel came closer. "Do you really want to let Rook down? After all of this? Do you want to let him die for nothing?"

Evan shook his head. He breathed deep and slow and even. It was then that he saw the second body lying at the side of the road. He crossed to it and saw that it was August. She looked like she was sleeping, but Evan sensed that she was not.

"The mean people got her too?" he asked.

"Yes," Gabriel said. "Even she was not safe. Please, Evan, there isn't much time. We must get you to the church. Do it for Rook."

Evan said, "Was it really what Rook wanted?"

"Yes. Truly."

Evan looked once more down at August. "Okay," he said, his voice small. "Where do we go?"

"Follow me."

Chapter Twenty-Five

They walked a ways through the woods and then came to a low clearing. Gabriel was ahead of Evan. Unable to explain it, Evan found himself wanting to imitate the man. He followed after him, walking where Gabriel walked, turning where Gabriel turned, wanting strangely to be like the man. *Rook's friend.*

The clearing ahead of them was flat with a slow depression leading to a frozen pond; on the other side more trees stood and a hill rose to a high ridge. Evan followed Gabriel around the pond. The pine trees were tall and thin, bare to an ash grey, but for the needles in the canopy. Across the forest floor there were many fallen, dead poplars and broken branches lying in half shadow. Yet for all of this they walked swiftly, almost gliding.

They went up the hill to the ridge. On the other side, another hill went back down to the forest floor, but there was an old worn walking trail between the slopes. They walked along it. A pale daylight reached them through the trees. Below the forest was hushed in gloom.

Gabriel paused. "How do you feel?" he asked.

Evan looked up at him. "I'm okay."

"Do you like this place, Evan?"

Evan surveyed the woods. "No. It's cold and it's dark."

Gabriel nodded. "That's very astute."

"A what?"

"I know that you feel you are different, Evan. You feel that you don't belong here."

Evan nodded, nudging a loose snow-dusted rock from the ground with his toe. It revealed a damp pocket of earth, and Evan imagined a grave. He moved his foot away.

"Can we keep going?" he asked.

"Of course."

They continued along the ridge in single file. The path sloped through a rock-strewn gully. Evan walked with his head down. They climbed once more to a new height facing due west and through the trees the sun was already beginning to set, a spreading murky red. To Evan it was the whole earth bleeding.

The hill opened up to a broad flattop. On every side there were wide views of the pine forest and a footpath leading below to the base of the ridge and far to the northeast the sound of the river over a patch of rapids carried up through the trees.

Gabriel stopped and stood straight. Beside him were the low stone ruins of a single four-walled structure. The area was grown over and choked with wild, leafless creeper vine and thickets along the edges.

Evan walked up from behind him. He remembered what Rook had told him: the church was just a bunch of old stone ruins.

"I don't get it," he said.

"You'll be safe once you go inside."

"But there's no walls."

"There are walls of another kind," Gabriel said. "Step inside, Evan. Inside you will be safe."

Evan walked up to the edge of the ruins and studied them, dubious. There appeared to be little concept of an inside at all. Even the remnant of the stone perimeter was incomplete, worn and weathered, leaving small gaps in its border.

He felt a sudden toxic aversion to it. To the smell of the soil and mossy stones. To the clinging static quality of the air. He felt the hairs on his neck standing on end, and it made him think if he put his hand over the boundary, lightning would strike him.

The failing sunlight was murky and reddish through the trees and Evan saw a glow appear in the ruins, enriched by the close shadow of the thicket. The stones seemed to hum in the light, as if the earth below was rumbling. Evan backed away.

"What's wrong?" Gabriel said.

"I don't like this place," Evan said.

Gabriel came close and reached out to place his hand on Evan's shoulder, but his hand stopped before it touched him. Evan flinched anyway.

Gabriel said, "Come with me."

He led Evan to the edge of the ridge where a rocky outcrop jutted over the slope, braced with wintered poplars.

"Sit," Gabriel said.

Evan sat. Gabriel joined him. They dangled their legs over the crag. Evan glanced back at the ruins and already he felt better being away from them. Then he looked at Gabriel. What early sense of menace he had felt was absent now. Instead, he was reminded of sitting with schoolteachers or with the counsellors at the orphanage. *A small office with an open window and a summer breeze of cut grass and sunlight and him seated quietly. Waiting to answer questions.*

For a while, Gabriel said nothing. The stone was cold under Evan's legs, but he sat still. He was happy to be still. He felt he had been running for as long as he could remember.

Finally, Gabriel said, "I don't like this place, either. It's a lonely place. It's a sad place. Don't you think?"

Evan nodded.

Gabriel asked, "Do you believe in Heaven?"

"I don't know. Sometimes."

"I believe in Heaven," Gabriel said. "In fact, I know it exists. It's a nice place. You don't have to be afraid or sad in Heaven. There are no questions. You just get to be. Doesn't that sound nice?"

Evan nodded. He was thinking about Rook.

"You miss Rook, don't you?" Gabriel said. "I miss him, too. And now you're all alone. He was all you had in this world, and now you have nothing. No friends. No family. No one even knows who you are. No one even knows if you're alive or dead. In a way, you might as well be dead. I mean, what more do you have to look forward to, here, except more sadness and darkness and pain?"

Gabriel paused and looked at Evan to judge his condition. Then he asked, "Wouldn't it be nice if you could just leave this place? Leave everything behind? Just like you have always wanted? Wouldn't that be better?"

Evan was quiet to his core. He sniffled against the cold.

"I can help you leave this place, Evan. I can take you someplace better. Away from all the pain and sadness and fear."

Evan looked up. "Where would we go?"

"Away from here. To a good place."

"Is that where Rook went?"

"Yes. Rook is there. And you can be with him again if you want."

"How do I get there?"

"Just step within those stones," Gabriel said, raising his arm. "Think of it as a doorway. All you have to do is open it."

Evan looked back at the ruins. Once more, he shuddered with an instinct for danger.

Gabriel sensed that the Adversary was close. *Now was the time*, he thought. He wished he could pick the child up and throw him into the boundary of the ruins, but that was impossible. The child had to enter of his own free will. Only then would the link to the Adversary be true.

Gabriel pursed his lips impatiently. He asked, "Haven't you wanted to know why you feel different, Evan? Why you feel separate from everyone else? Why you can sense people like they are animals below you? Haven't you wanted to know why you can feel people's pain and sadness in your head? Don't you want to know who you are?"

Evan said, "I want to go wherever Rook is."

"Then all you have to do is step within the stones, Evan, and you can be with him forever. All of this will go away. It will just be you and Rook."

Evan wiped his cheeks. "I didn't want him to leave," he said.

"And you can have him back. He's waiting for you."

Once more, Evan looked back at the ruins.

"I just go in there?" he asked.

"That's all. Just step over the stones."

"And I'll get to be with Rook?"

"Yes."

Evan nodded. "Okay," he said, and he stood.

Gabriel stood as well. He looked down at Evan. "It will be better, Evan. Everything will be better. I swear. Go on."

Evan walked to the edge of the ruins. He still had that sense of danger, but decided to ignore it. Fear and pain didn't matter anymore. There was nothing. He just wanted to be with Rook.

He stepped over the stone boundary.

As soon as he was standing on the ground within the ruins, the cold air of the forest lifted away. Evan's head filled with lightness like he had stood up too fast. He drifted forward. Then he stepped back. He looked down and the earth was rising up to meet him and he put his hands out to stop it.

Evan crashed hard to the frozen ground. He was down on his hands and knees. He trembled and opened his mouth to breathe but the air was hot and wet and it stuck in his throat.

Something bad is happening, he thought. *Something very bad is happening.*

All at once, he started sweating under his clothes and his stomach turned over like he was about to vomit. His heartbeat pounded in his chest. His skin prickled and burned and his bones ached.

Gabriel stepped to the edge of the ruins and looked down at Evan. His expression was smooth and contented and serene. He listened to the child begin to scream.

Evan lay curled in a fetal position, then kicking his legs out only to pull them in again. He could hear a voice calling him, vague and distant. Calling out his name.

Twisting, he gritted his teeth against another scream and buried his face in the ground, which was now moist and soft under him. Again, from a distance, he heard someone calling his name.

"Rook!" he cried.

"Rook cannot protect you anymore," Gabriel said. "Let it happen, child."

Evan flipped over and lay flat on his back. His breath boiled in his throat and steam spurted from his open mouth as he gasped and choked.

"Do not resist. It will be easier for you."

The heat poured out of him, closing over his body like a tomb. Then his vision dimmed and he saw only flashes of white upon black, sharp images of a creature crawling along a stone-strewn shore.

At that moment, a burst of fire leapt from Evan's mouth and with the flame arose a voice. *A scream.* Evan heard it and was surprised because it was not his own. It was the voice of some other being within him and it screamed with a pitch of such clear agony and fury together that it sounded almost beautiful in its purity.

Gabriel lifted his chin, angling his gaze so he could better look down upon the scene. He knew the final moment was near. The Adversary was found.

Evan's eyes were closed. His pulse throbbed massively in his head and at the same time he could feel it outside himself. As if someone drove a heavy hammer against the earth right next to him. All around, it was spreading. The wet ground beat with the same rhythm of his heart, the small stones jumped with it, the pools of melted snow rippled. And then, coming from afar, rising up, he heard the clear calling of his name.

The voice shared the same intensity as the scream he had heard, and it was right at his ear, as if someone lay, alive and real, on the ground beside him.

"Evan! Evan! Hear me!"

He wished with all his soul that it was Rook, but he knew it wasn't.

Evan recognized this voice now. It was the voice that spoke through him when he used his special-thinking. It was the voice that had helped him carry Rook from the cornfield to safety. It was the voice of his heart's double beat.

"You are being tricked, Evan. The pain you think you feel is false. You are okay. What lives in these stones can't hurt a human child. It means to confuse you, to keep you in the light while they search for me. It is my pain you feel, Evan, not your own. But if they catch me we will both perish. Do you understand this? You must see through the pain, Evan. You must stand up and get out of here."

Evan cried out and his shoulder blades struck the ground as his back arched in a savage contortion.

". . . I can't! I can't!"

"You must, Evan. I know you are afraid. I know you wish someone would come and lift you up and take you away from this. We have always been hunted, chased, hated and feared and driven against a wall, but that is our great burden. And there is no bright light above that can save us. I didn't want you to learn of our bond like this. I wanted you to learn in time. But we must save ourselves now. And we can, Evan, if we help each other. I need you to stand up and get outside these stones."

Slowly, Evan turned on his side tried to stand. Then he went down again.

". . . It hurts too much!"

"You are strong, Evan. That's why I chose you. You must get us outside the stones. I will do the rest. Trust me."

And then the voice that spoke from Evan's heart said, *"Evan, these people that have tricked us, that have hunted us, that are trying to destroy us now, they were the ones that tricked Rook. They were the ones who killed him."*

At that moment, Evan's chest kicked and his eyes opened. He saw the surrounding forest in a haze of rust-coloured bursts and flares, and then he saw Gabriel standing at the edge of the stones and his focus sharpened like he was staring down a tunnel.

He felt the scream rise up his throat as a spurt of fire, only this time it was his own. "You killed Rook!"

Gabriel stepped back from the stones, away from the piercing shriek of the child. His jaw clenching with sudden panic, as he watched the child turn over and start crawling, his fingers digging into the almost muddy earth, dragging himself to the edge of the stones.

"No, you can't!" Gabriel shouted. Desperation overcame him. He ran to the edge of the ruins and lifted his leg to kick Evan back within the boundary. As his foot came down on Evan's head, there was a bright flash of blue light and Gabriel's kick rebounded and he flew backwards. His foot had been pulverized. Evan kept crawling.

"There is a great power inside of us. . . ."

With both hands Evan gripped one of the old stones and dragged himself up, his cheek resting upon it.

"We are the shadow and the fire and the night. . . ."

His chest slid across the smooth top of the stone, then his belly, and at last he slipped over onto the cold flat earth beyond.

"We are the power of darkness. Now, we have become."

Chapter Twenty-Six

Evan gasped and the cold air drew him back and he felt the solidity of the earth under him where he lay. A beautiful and even warmth encased him. His heartbeat was like a drum keeping time. A single beat, calm and clear.

There were curious thoughts in his head, vague memories slowly coming to clarity, a world of things he had not even known he'd forgotten. A sudden impression of belonging overwhelmed him, as of a home bidding him welcome, and he rolled his head and looked up at Gabriel. He *knew* him.

"Hello, brother," he said, his voice smooth and old, yet still childlike.

Lying on the ground unable to stand, concealing grimaces of pain, Gabriel watched as Evan got to his knees, and then to his feet.

"No . . ." Gabriel stammered. "You cannot . . . We had you in the light."

Evan regarded Gabriel with a slight tilt of his head. Then he started around the edge of the stones. He walked with a casual air, light in the snow like a kid swinging his feet through piles of leaves. When he reached Gabriel's side of the ruins, he stopped and regarded Gabriel's destroyed foot.

"Did your pride get the best of you?" he asked, with a playful grin. "It's against an angel's nature to interfere physically in this world. You know that."

Gabriel glared at him with loathing. Evan laughed and then sat down.

"You won't win," Gabriel said.

Evan ignored him. He was busy digging his fingers into the snow between his feet, amazed at how easily he could dig down into the frozen ground beneath. His hand cut through the dirt and rock like a knife through butter. After a moment, he raised his hand with a dark clump of snow and dirt clutched in it. He admired the cold earth.

"It's breathtaking, isn't it?" he said. His fist closed tightly, grinding the earth to coat his fingers and palm.

For a split second, Gabriel noticed himself drifting. As if in a trance, he wanted to agree with Evan, to sit at his feet and marvel at the magnificence of things.

"You snake!" he snapped, shaking himself. "I'd never join you."

Evan shrugged. "Okay."

"Our patience is eternal," Gabriel said. "You may have snuck into this kingdom, but you will never find peace here. Here, they *hate* you. They will hunt you, and one day you will be outcast once again. Then we will come for you."

Evan looked across at Gabriel. "We'll see," he said. "I don't think they hate me as much as you'd like to believe. You see they *need* to hate me so that they can try to be good people. But we'll see. Either way, I've never expected you or our brothers to understand the mission Father asked of me. It was always mine to carry alone."

"How dare you speak of our Father?"

Ignoring Gabriel's admonition, Evan brought his dirt-stained hand to his mouth and bit down hard on the space between his thumb and forefinger. Blood came into his mouth. He jerked his hand away viciously and waved his arm through the air to spray his blood upon the ground.

All at once, the snow and ice beneath Gabriel began to melt. He hauled himself up, but only to his knees. He understood quickly that the heat was inescapable. It was coming from within him. Sweat beaded on his brow, but he settled into it with a stoic expression. He knew he had lost this time, but he wouldn't give Evan the satisfaction of seeing him squirm. Still, he began to breathe raggedly. Steam rose from under his jacket. And then in a sudden bright burst, Gabriel erupted in a whirlwind of flame.

He reeled back but the fire was inside him, and burned off him in swirling plumes.

Evan got to his feet, watching, his eyes reflecting the flames. The fire leapt into the surrounding brush and spread, chasing the tangles of wild vine and charring the wintered poplars. Then Gabriel collapsed.

Evan watched Gabriel's clothing sizzle and melt to his skin, blackened and boiling. He went forward, tried to look Gabriel in the eyes, but his face was hardly more than a burned-out hole. A putrid smell filled the forest as the body's innards roasted.

An iridescent light filled the woods. It had sprung up and out of Gabriel's burning carcass and cast off, shining through the heights of the pine trees above the fire.

Evan watched the light depart, and within it he saw the glimmer of many soaring wings. A small part of his heart went out to them, remembering what it was like to soar in their company. He realized they had come to witness his destruction, Gabriel acting only as their physical messenger, their voice.

He watched their light cut through the dark in swift diminishing flight and thought, *Not yet, brothers, not yet*. Then the light was gone. The forest darkened.

Evan looked down at the burned and smoldering lump that had been Gabriel's earthly body and he wondered, in a moment's sadness, whom it was that he had truly burned. What poor soul had offered Gabriel the use of his body, and in exchange for what?

Evan shuddered. He examined the wound he had given himself, blood clotted and dried. He raised his hand to his mouth and sucked.

All at once, what flames were left extinguished into smoke. Everything hissed. A wind rose and the trees creaked and smoked with a hushed simmering, and below, there carried the faraway noise of the river.

Evan stood with his arms at his sides. He watched the smoke swirl and rise and dissipate into the night. Then he closed his eyes. When he opened them again, his irises were a deep, charcoal black. He walked along the burned ridge and down through the woods, descending from a cloud of smoke.

When he reached the edge of the trees he crossed the ditch and went up onto the road. His legs were covered in snow and he stood breathing grey plumes out of his mouth. He could smell the sweet charred richness of the burned wood in the air. He stared up at the dark and star-filled sky and watched the smoke drift like it was a low cloud. Then he turned and walked along the shoulder of the road.

Evan saw the outline of the truck in the moonlight and stopped. He considered turning around and walking the other way. He could see the bulk of the hood and the cab and the sheen of moonlight on the windshield. All the rest lay in shadow. After a moment he continued walking.

A small part of him was expecting—hoping—to find the truck abandoned and Rook gone. Maybe he would never see him again, but at least he would know he was alive, somewhere. He stopped when he saw the outline of Rook's body.

He was still against the grill of the truck. More snow had swept from across the field and Rook was covered as if under a winding sheet.

Evan looked down at him, his eyes welling up. Then his expression softened and he felt the warmth of tears running on his cheeks. He let them fall.

"I remember when you called out that night," he said. "You were really sad. I could hear it like someone was tolling a bell, and it made ripples go across the lake. I had to find you. I had to answer. But all I did was make you suffer more. I forced you to go on living without your goodness. I'm sorry, Rook."

Evan glanced once at the dark shape that lay on the side of the road.

"I am the Lord of all that is mean and bad in this world, but I love this world, too, as my Father does. I want this world to know my Father's goodness. It is *all*. That is why I carry the burden of evil. For Him. For you."

Coming down the road in the dark, Evan saw yellow headlights.

"I really wish you would talk to me," he said. "I miss the sound of your voice. It's hard to believe after all this you're actually gone. *Are you?*"

He focused his thoughts on Rook in his special way. He could feel that his powers were stronger now. Strong enough, perhaps, to bring him back.

He waited and listened, hoping to hear Rook's voice, hoping to feel it move through him, but there was nothing.

The being that had been Evan hung his head. He backed away from Rook's body and turned towards the road. The headlights were still far off but they were growing closer. He started walking towards them and as he rounded the end of the truck, he paused and looked over his shoulder. He wanted to say—

But there were no more words. Evan turned back and walked along the middle of the road. He put his hands inside his pants' pockets and hung his head. The illusion that he was just a child returned.

Eventually, the headlights washed over him and he looked up into the blinding glare. The car slowed down, then stopped.

The doors opened. A woman's voice called to him. He heard her heels clicking on the road. Then he saw her appear between the headlights. When she knelt in front of him, Evan looked at the ground. He felt all at once like a child again. From over the glare of the headlights a man called out.

"Is he all right?"

"What's your name, sweetheart? Are you okay?" the woman asked. She lifted his chin. She saw the streaks of tears and soot on his face and looked into his charcoal-coloured eyes. They startled her, but she forced a smile. She struggled to imagine what in the world a child was doing out in the middle of nowhere.

"Hey hon, what's your name?"

"Mary, is he all right?" the man called.

"Are you out here all alone?"

Evan said nothing.

The woman took his hand and led him to the car. She opened the back seat and Evan climbed inside.

"He's out here all alone," she said to the man.

"Yeah," he said. "There's a truck up there, and it smells like there's been a fire."

"I'll call 911."

"Hang on," the man said. "I don't want to be waiting out here for an hour. We'll call when we get home."

"Can we do that? What about the boy?"

"Well, I guess we'll take him somewhere."

"Well, we can't just leave him."

"No, we can't."

The woman closed the rear door and came around to the passenger seat and got in. They were about to drive when the man stopped.

"Hang on," he said. "Look, there's someone else on the road over there."

The man opened his door and got out.

"Joe!" the woman said anxiously. She turned around in her seat and looked at Evan. "Everything's going to be all right," she said.

From outside the car, the man called. "Mary, come here! It's a lady, maybe the kid's mother. She's unconscious, but she's breathing."

The woman glanced once more at Evan, gave a quick reassuring smile, and then opened her door and stepped out.

Evan watched the woman cross in front of the car's headlights into the dark.

August, he thought. *She's alive. Good. She will help me.*

After a moment, the back door opened and the man leaned in with August in his arms.

"Careful," the woman said over his shoulder. "Her leg's broken."

Evan moved over to give August room, as the man laid her across the seat. She looked strangely peaceful. The skin around her eyes was bright pink and fresh like when a scab falls off.

The couple closed the door and then got into the front. They spoke again about calling 911, but Evan wasn't listening. The car started forward and drove past the truck.

Evan watched the night flowing over the windshield and he smelled the wood smoke of the forest. It made him think of cold stone and running through snow. His eyes welled up again and his chest and throat began to burn. He moved closer to August.

The farther away they drove, the more terribly he smelled smoke and stone and the harder that place in his heart wrenched with a hollowing pain.

So this is humanity.

He sat up a bit and turned around to look out the rear window, expecting something, but he saw only the dark road in the red of the taillights.

ACKNOWLEDGEMENTS

Thank you to my ChiZine family: Brett Savory for being a wonderful risk taker; Sandra Kasturi for bringing this book to life and making me a stronger writer along the way; Samantha Beiko and Leigh Teetzel for your thoughtful and constructive edits and proofreads; Jared Shapiro for the beautiful interior design; and Erik Mohr for the awesome book cover. Thanks to Michael Rowe, my writing mentor, whose early notes helped turn this story from a cringeworthy cliché into something a little more honest. Thanks to my mom, dad, and sister, who have always acknowledged my writing with tremendous encouragement and support, and my brother, Michael Michell, whose daily inspiration is pretty much the only reason why I do any of this. And thank you to whoever is reading this sentence. I hope you enjoyed the book.

About The Author

Stephen Michell lives and works in Toronto, Ontario as a freelance writer. He has published a few short stories in various journals, magazines, and anthologies. *Only the Devil Is Here* is his first novel. Find out more about him at stephenmichell.com or follow him on Instagram @sopmichell.